Love Song of the Australopiths

by

Tito Perdue

Books by Tito Perdue

Lee (1991)
The New Austerities (1994)
Opportunities in Alabama Agriculture (1994)
The Sweet-Scented Manuscript (2004)
Fields of Asphodel (2007)
The Node (2011)
Morning Crafts (2013)
Reuben (2014)
The Builder: William's House I (2016)
The Churl: William's House II (2016)
The Engineer: William's House III (2016)
The Bachelor: William's House IV (2016)
Cynosura (2017)
Philip (2017)
Though We Be Dead, Yet Our Day Will Come (2018)
The Bent Pyramid (2018)
The Philatelist (2018)
The Smut Book (2018)
The Gizmo (2019)

Love Song of the Australopiths

by

Tito Perdue

Standard American Publishing Company-
Brent, Alabama
2020

Cover image: Detail from
The Lion of the Season, Punch, May 25, 1861

Cover design by: Kevin Slaughter

Hardcover ISBN: 978-1-940933-70-2
Paperback ISBN: 978-1-940933-71-9
E-book ISBN: 978-1-940933-72-6

CONTENTS

"Intoxicated with animosity"—Macaulay

One

As you know, I've spent most of this past week in anti-Semitic activities, and it's time to turn in my report. You know, too, how much I adore my own Aryan genetics, my antecedents, and the list of accomplishments those of us have wrought. But first, I want to cite some of the recruits who in recent days have pledged themselves to our incipient (if all-too-slowly-unfolding) revolution.

I name *Taw Billingsly* (not his real name) an anti-Semitic gunsmith, handwriting expert, and documentarian of the first degree. About 15% longer than your customary white male's, the major digits on his right paw (alpha and beta, he calls them) are warped, as it were, and run off at angles painful to see. ("Paw," we say, because of certain other qualities of his to be described later on, time and energy permitting.)

I have seen this man reprogram 3-D printers and replicate driver licenses in perfect authenticity with the aid of quantum scanners specializing in tasks of this sort. I have seen him produce pharmaceutical prescriptions of perfect authenticity as also citizenship papers, automobile plates, small currencies, and the airline ticket he had needed to absent himself from Baltimore. I have heard, though not yet seen, how he has forwarded some of that ersatz money, most of it really, to the organization that will comprise the central subject of this just-begun account that is expected to need about 200 pages typed. I shall not, however, attempt to describe this man's appearance beyond mentioning that it corresponds precisely to the likely preconception of those with good intuition who in addition have had connections with others of this type, as haven't we all?

It is to this person that I owe my placebos, my passports, three credit cards, *all* of my drivers' licenses, and a ready supply of European and American small bills. In candor, I'm not absolutely certain our little movement

could continue without him. I last visited with him on
Friday, congregating at his lake-side home with some nine
or ten other activists who hadn't come together for a
month or more. Old revolutionists, you must understand,
are generally the *best* revolutionists. We need young ones,
too, of course we do, but it is we septuagenarians and better who have so much the less to fear and need not explain why we be unemployed or so often found wandering
city streets when we ought to be in bed.

We dined on ribs and ale after which the counterfeiter
called in his wife to receive our thanks. She ate separately
and never sought to mix with intellectual matters. And in
short—she *was* rather short—she was by much the most
adored woman in the organization.

"Thank you, dear," said the host after we had delivered
our appreciation for the meal. "And now, we'll let you get
back to whatever you were doing."

Would only someday I might have a wife such as she!
With hardly a decade still in escrow, I need someone to
wake me each noon and flatter me at intervals during the
lengthening afternoons.

In this man's house, we drank ale instead of beer. The
table was long and heavy, and among the floor-to-ceiling
shelving were many hundreds of thick-looking books in
leather covers. Outside, the day was fading like an antique
photograph, the labile sun retreating ever more hastily as
the minutes went past. From far away, a dog was calling
with decaying enthusiasm, uncertain whether to go on
with it or not. My host and collaborator, an unhealthy
man, coughed twice into his napkin and deposited it in his
pocket. We were all of us unhealthy, most of us, a propitious condition for "turning weakness into strength," as
we liked to say. On that premise, the man to my right was
strongest of all.

For me, it was the best moment of the week—a select
group of select men debating seriously into the late after-

noon. We judged time by the sound of crickets and children splashing in the lake. "Must be past nine o'clock," I mooted. I've always been good with time, all the more so as time becomes scarcer for me, my friends, and I.

Two

When as on the first day of the world, I rose early and went to host the sun. Normal people, those that remain, had been up for hours already and going about their duties, which is to say pacing back to work and forth, making telephone calls, selling insurance policies, or keeping computers in repair. I love them and rely upon them but had rather be dead than made to give attention to such matters. Music and crime, old books and landscape scenes, only these and kindred things hold *my* interest.

I breakfasted on toast and coffee and not much else. Came then a call from someone in a foreign accent offering a discounted rate on a ten-day vacation in the Bahamas. And did my grandfather, a man of integrity, even know of such a place? I do try to be polite to people, however.

"No, thank you," I replied. "Goodbye."

I knew she wouldn't stop. It was, of course, a negress, obviously tired of having to read the same script over and over. My grandfather would have been incensed by such a person using a telephone, but I endured it.

The second call came immediately after, a male this time, seeking Toby.

"Not here," I said.

"Gotta be."

"Sorry."

"And just who might *you* be?"

It was to be a long hard twenty-first-century day, and I tried to prepare for it. Came then the third call, a request for funding by the B'nai Brith. It was not a modern machine, my telephone, and even apart from all the buildings and other obstructions in these parts, the voice was highly discontinuous and mixed with static. It came from some other part of New York City.

I dressed, foddered the dog, and then leapt to saddle and started the engine. I have the funds for a better car, but when I bethought me of the paperwork, the gas and oil, insurance and tire pressure, I much prefer to *will* myself to places than have to travel there. And then there were those *license plates* that have to be renewed each year. Once, once only had I been given a tag number (1715) easy to remember on account of a famous historical date. Today's date was not five per-cent finished and already the blatant sun was exposing every defect in my vicinity. I will say it just once, that people, if they be wise, will wish to be awake only when the world is black and quiet and propitious for books and concerts and the rest.

I drove for a certain number of blocks (I do sometimes wear Halloween masks when driving) trying to store up in memory the look and feel of our contemporary age. The buildings, rectangular products with windows in them, are likely just as good as those of old-time Sogdiana or Medieval Japan. I don't mean to insult my own epoch, and in truth I don't suppose life was any better in Hellas when things were at their all-times best. Except for a profound variance in cultural development, the people were likely just the same. Depressed by this, I was startled just then to see a jigaboo in a parking lot micturating in someone's gas tank. Two blocks further, I descried an interracial couple who from the look of things were colluding already. Spitting in the gene pool! I wanted to puke. And how would *you* like it—to catch view of a pretty little white person copulating with a housefly? There were more ill-featured people here fore and aft than in the Book of Moses. Saw I then a comely woman in a brief skirt who in previous years might have caused me to look again; instead, today, I rounded the corner, parked, and indulged a few moments of light-grade sleep. I also wanted to hear the last few measures of Maher's Eighth playing on the machine.

I needed to piss. The world was old, the buildings old, too, but older still is the magnetic core that gives the world its gyroscopic focus. And that's how old are *we*, my friends and me.

I had brought along my expired plate, the vehicle identification number, my driver's license with its passport-size photograph, a set of fingerprints and DNA diagram, but in spite of all that I was not immediately allowed to have new tags. I had expected this. Very seldom these days do my ventures meet with success on even the second or third attempts. The clerk (and I do not blame *her* for the modern world) was trying earnestly to earn her pay and after eight hours return home where for an hour or two, and if she wasn't too tired, life was possible. I smiled sympathetically. She was maybe fifty years in age, and her upper arms were turning into butter, but I liked her even so. How many good and bad children had she not brought into the world, how many meals and knitted sweaters for her lout of a husband?

"Not your fault," I said. "It's just the way things are these days. Let him fix his own goddamn breakfast. Me, I'll just toddle on over to the insurance place and bring things up to date."

She agreed to it. The insurance place was in Queens, a district named after the sort of people who live there. I found myself forced to drive without insurance and plates through hellish traffic for a distance greater than that 'tween Thebes and Athens. The faces I saw, the bright shiny new cars, the ethnic districts—I tried to photograph all this with my mind in order later on to make a gift of it to the historians yet to come. But would they believe me? I counted nine constipated and/or pregnant negresses preparing to unburden themselves on the sidewalk. From all around, aboriginal music filled the air. Naturally, this was the moment for me to bump into the SUV in front of me and produce a dent, a tiny one, in his or her ornamented fender, a trivial incidence that in normal times would not have deserved the ink to mention it.

It was a smallish man, him who speedily abandoned his vehicle and put himself where either I must drive over him or else park my Romanian car and go to meet him. He was sizzling.

"You're a menace on the highway!" he revealed. "Hey! What am I, just another little *mischling* to you people? You should be locked up!"

I remained polite, the best subterfuge in New York City. Old I may be, yet I could and probably should have messed up his face a little bit.

"Terribly sorry. But it doesn't seem to have done any harm."

"Harm? What did you say? You want harm, I'll call my brother!"

"But I can't even see any damage."

"Can't see it? Like you can't see it, then it's not there, is that what it is? We don't got no air, right, 'cause you can't see it?"

We exchanged insurance information, the rectum too furious to note how out-of-date was mine. His car, black and about eighteen rods long, gasped and heaved and managed finally to turn at Marcus Garvey and MLK. Pleased to be shut of him, I extracted Mahler and threw something of Shostakovich's on the machine. You want contrast? Listen to good music while driving through New York City. Having no tag (not to mention insurance) a policeman now brought me to a halt in the middle of Jellyroll Morton Avenue. God, he was a large man, his naval at the level of my face and his head, unmistakably shaped, lost in the sun. Mesmerized by his odor, I took out my license and showed it to him. Where was my Muffler Inspection Receipt, he asked, and was I carrying firearms on board? I had forgot that I was.

I followed him slowly for a distance greater than the crow-flight from Athens to Troezen. But it was my music I think that most incensed the man. My Smith & Wesson he transferred to his own evil car that boasted an engine far more powerful, I'm quite sure, than my East European one. The police station, a utilitarian structure, was full of noise and tens and tens of a characteristic sort of people. Adorning myself in sheepish smiles, I interviewed the man behind the desk. A scuffle had broken out in the ante-chamber and for one precious moment I entertained the notion of escaping. The stench in that place had certifiably an ethnic dimension.

In the end, I paid $840 dollars together with taxes, fines, environment protection adjustments, and my Smith & Wesson. He promised to take good care of it.

By contrast, the insurance place contained a better class of people, somewhat better, waiting on benches. It's hard for me to remember that I need six several credentials to use my own car. My grandfather, how many credentials had *he* carried and would I have liked that person if I had known him? Deprived of today's labor-saving devices, he had wasted the better share of his life simply earning a living. Let me explain further that I have a persistent pain in my left liver and would have wanted to lie down if I but could. But couldn't. I *was* able to identify the men's room but by no means could I afford to sacrifice my place on the bench. In old times, a man might strike up a conversation to while away the time. But that was long ago and far away. Here, it was 11:25 in New York City.

In the end, I invested in liability insurance while scanting the cost of coverage for damage to my own vehicle. I could buy another car but the last I wanted was to pay the hospital costs of those who ran into me. And then, too, this time the clerk was a male even if not however a terribly good one. He did have an artful tattoo on his neck to show that his carotid had been sliced open and that he was bleeding out.

"Jesus Christ man, you been going without insurance *for three months*? Fuck, man, you're lucky no one crashed into you!"

"Naw, I carry a gun."

He laughed. He was not a bad type really. Might have made a Confederate grenadier, had he come forth at the right time and place. I estimated him a Scandinavian of some type, other ingredients notwithstanding.

I paid, took the chit, and wended my way out of a crowd consisting of very unlike economic classes of human beings. The district was wretchedly poor, judging from this group, or else composed overwhelmingly of people too ignorant to keep their insurance up to date. I had chosen to ignore the half-dozen calls on my mobile telephone though one of them appeared to be valid. Once outside, I accessed the good one and chatted at length with a colleague soliciting funds for a right-wing periodical. I listened patiently. I had given almost $60,000 already but might do more if John Morgan could be inveigled on board.

I have not bothered to mention that this city is at all times full of noise and that this account was perforce set down amid a hailstorm of ambulances, cell phone alerts, babies, brakes and doors, gunshots, and feet punching holes in sidewalks, a paradise for extroverts. I drove over that enormous magma chamber recently discovered some eight miles beneath the intersection of Moab and Seventh Avenue. Would night never come? Suddenly I stopped, very nearly running over a white woman of decent appearance. The town had by now passed over into afternoon, and the people, recently victualed, were snoozing on their feet.

Stop here, if you don't care for reportage of this kind.

Three

Three weeks almost went by before I visited my fourth-favorite collaborator, a six-foot four-inch individual with an I.Q. even taller. I knew him to have already slain at least one of our domestic enemies while leaving behind not the least evidence of anything. All they knew, the journalists, was that one of their number was missing. How did he do it, this dear friend of mine? You aren't ready for that. I shall always remember him as *Lloyd Vanderslice,* which is about as far as possible from his actual name.

I entered with trepidation, saluted the other guests, most of them friends of mine, and then lapsed onto a sofa upholstered in a high-grade paisley framed in teak. Educated in dentistry at Emory University, this remarkable individual had volunteered his service to the M'Baka Tribe in the Central African Republic, a place therebefore destitute of oral and maxillofacial surgeons. We do not know the number of those healed by him, children and adults suffering from tribal disagreements. He seems to have felt some satisfaction in what he was doing and even endured a serious viral infection vectored by his patients. But after a certain while, his optimism began to wane. The dog he had adopted was taken by the children, hung, dissected, and left on his front porch. Having refused one of the prostitutes, her husband attacked him with a machete and two days following that, the better part of his equipment was stolen, bringing an effective halt to his efforts. Meantime, he had received a peremptory message from the sponsoring United Nations agency criticizing him vehemently for the insensitivity he had displayed during his sojourn. A progressive senator had proposed that he not be allowed to return to his erstwhile country, and his son, a scholarship student at M.I.T. had written to say that their relationship had ended. Resigned to it, he was preparing to leave the continent when an incursion of some twelve-hundred Sara tribesmen descended on the place and after slaughtering the males and older females, seized upon my friend and carried him off as a light-skin curiosity of especial value.

I know nothing of these transactions save that he was quickly married off to a 400-pound maiden related to the Economics Minister of a breakaway province to the northeast of his new address. He found some favor there owing to his medicines and skill in maintaining the special dentition of the warrior class. If he wished to retain that favor (and his life) he was expected (required) to take part in the raids underway against the tribe's Gbaya-speaking enemies, ghastly specimens now threatening from the west. Urged by his experience of Africa and its people, he declared himself keen to do so. Appointed commander of a "battalion," of Zande "troops," the *New York Paper* accredited him with 2,600-3,000 black demises over the course of just 110 days. We had no trouble recruiting him to our cause.

"My plane was held up in Rome," he said, once the meeting got under way, "but Frank might be joining us later."

But he never did, Frank, join us later, and it wasn't till three days later we learned he had been arrested. I listened quietly as our host then went over our accounts and introduced the individual he had selected for the editorship of our proposed quarterly. A man of somewhat less than average height, largely bald, his was an astringent-looking face betokening, I believed, a resolute nature and high intelligence. A dead cigarette floated in his half-empty coffee cup, and his glasses, or one lens anyway, had a fog on it. A nervous fellow, we realized right away.

He had edited other journals in the past, one of them, *The Albion Review*, an intellectual organ of some distinction that was ruined after just two-and-a-half years by the inadequate number of subscribers combined with increas-

ing postal rates. He had tried, uselessly, to be given a sub-
vention from one or two wealthy readers but had perforce
to shut down the enterprise just as it was beginning to
gather a sustainable readership. To earn money, he then
put out an expensive, too expensive as it proved, book of
colored photographs of notable European landscape scenes.
This, too, failed, leaving him in near-penury. We have always wanted the most prosperous people we could find,
though in his case we were ready to take experience and his
well-attested history of anti-Semitism in lieu of wealth.

Our own prosperity was doing well. Some years earlier
we had bought a grocery in a negro neighborhood and
had reinvested the very considerable profits in the initial
offering of a biotech micro-startup focusing on the genetic
repair of the lipid system. A propitious investment, we
sold our shares soon after for a net profit of just under six
million. To avert the capital gains penalty, the money was
quickly reinvested in a television studio promoting the
interests of the Aryan community. And then, too, one of
our sympathizers, a California bond scammer, has written
us into his last will and testament. We cannot know how
much might finally accrue to us but expect it to be an appreciable sum indeed.

We adjourned to allow the old folks—most of us are
old—to visit the toilet. Even here, a stack of newspapers
and magazines lay ready to hand, demonstrating how
alert we are, those of our sort, to misinformation. We keep
abreast of our enemies. Or insofar as that is possible when
our enemies own such a great part of the country's attention.

His book collection, Lloyd's, enthralled me. I had wandered into the library and was critiquing the four or five
dozen Hungarian imprints that for the first time gave me
some hint as to the man's origins and pedigree. We are a
secretive people, of course, and have no alternative but to
seek anonymity. Permitted to smoke in this place, I con-

sumed my first cigarette in two days while at the same time browsing through a rather fatigued copy of the second edition of the *Fulminations* of 1821, a hard-core Rosicrucian disquisition I recommend to no one. That was when the brain-drained editor listed above came and sat across from me. He was utilizing cough drops as also a goblet wherein a fluid of some sort drifted slowly back and forth. A bent cigarette, trembling visibly, protruded from the left corner of his bright red lips. And in short, he was much as I have described him.

"Good book?" he inquired pleasantly, rising to view the text. The effort broke the ash on his cigarette which fell to his knee and resided there.

"No, no, no. A very bad one," I courteously replied.

"But we must keep abreast of our enemies, no?"

I looked at him. There are certain people in this world, mind-readers, who can do things like this. I moved back a few inches.

"So!" I said, wanting to clear the air. "We have the resources, you think, to put out a new quarterly?"

"You don't think I dropped those ashes on purpose!"

"No, no." (My God, he was odd.)

"Could we start with a million?" I innocently inquired. "Enough to sign with a printer? Postal costs? Should we take advertising? And writers, do we have the writers?"

"I'll have the writers when you have the million."

"But we do have it."

"You say that?" He moved closer.

"Of course. You'll have to be bonded, needless to say."

"Ah. I was waiting for that. What about my house? Should I take out a third mortgage?"

"You already have. But we haven't discussed that apartment in Jersey. In your wife's name I believe?"

(I adore the expression on people's face when they realize just how up-to-date we be.)

We reconvened at eleven. Two further anti-Semites

had belatedly joined us including notably a Finnish individual who spoke one language only and it with an accent. His story, I later learned, had to do with certain actions the Bolsheviks had carried out against his grandparents a hundred years ago in southeast Finland. Tonight, he had brought along a briefcase full of printed material and was continually lurching forward during the discussions as if he wished to speak but couldn't.

Now the other late-comer, Fred Reeves, is an ordinary-seeming type to be described in much greater detail when we come to that part. About some seventy years in age, the man is faintly humpback and wears an odious moustache employed primarily for straining liquid foods. I don't believe I've ever seen him without some little tad of something or another caught in the bristles of that unneeded accoutrement.

The personality seated just next to him—myself—is two inches shorter than he used to be. In comparison with the Finn, he speaks fluently if not indeed too often. His book collection is quite good and even now he can bench-press just slightly less than half his own weight. After all those years, he has turned out to be quite a prosperous and even a respectable citizen with a dog, a twelve-room apartment (for a single person, twelve is an indulgence almost), and a "powerful red car," as Nabokov said. Having labored for more than five years in a tall office building on lower Broadway, he had invested his savings with a Jewish street broker adept at arbitraging short-sales of Middle Eastern currencies. Retired by forty-one, he (I), began a program of serious readings that brought him to my current development.

I shall discuss this man's wives, his three overlapping marriages, when we arrive at that. Admit it, the third marriage was a mistake and ought never have been undertaken. I never knew that woman's full genealogy and could not have anticipated the sort of offspring she was bound to bring forward. She lives now in Miami with her children who all look very much alike as I've been told. But it was my second wife, an improved reification who deserves a marginally more favorable reference. I shall attend to that later on.

In regard to your other questions, I should explain that generally I sleep throughout the day coming awake only after the moon has made its appearance in my tiny window. No one can encroach upon me when I'm sleeping although it *has* been tried on one occasion at least. He had imagined, the malefactor, that he could cut through the bars with a corrugated wire passed back and forth repeatedly over the course of weeks. A white person would have known better. No doubt he was after my stamp collection, my most precious possession, fully insured, kept in perfect protection at The Bank of New York.

You'll want to understand that I eat just once a day, or night rather, usually at around 2:00 in the morning. Truth is, I abominate the whole procedure, a waste of time analogous to a bowel movement seen from the obverse angle of view. I will eat olives and mushrooms and a few other things. I do drink wine, inexpensive stuff as I cannot distinguish the good, so-denominated, from the bad. Alright, I prefer rosé, particularly in view of the view of it when held up to the light. One can see *layers* in there, rather like a geological cross section where the liquid has separated, so to speak, in accord with density, age, and atomic structure. An expert can identify the various vintages in a glass of that stuff. The taste is alright, too.

What else? My book hoard is not perhaps as valuable as my stamps though I do possess a half-dozen incunabula and a certain number of early sixteenth-century imprints identified by me from Foib's 1887 *Perpetuity Catalog,* so-called. My book dealer, as unscrupulous a person as you'd ever wish to meet, adores me. Books are furniture, too, but now my library is nearly full. All this, you understand, comes to me from the stock and futures markets, Jewish inventions that allow me to countervail against them. I will not buy a book until I have invested a certain sum in anti-Semitic activities.

About this, more later. By 11:30, just as I was coming awake, we adjourned the meeting and went our separate ways. He shook with each of us, did Lloyd, and offered parting gifts of chocolate wafers from Switzerland. I prefer to walk at times like these—my apartment is just seven blocks away, and I will take my chances with street niggers before setting foot in a taxicab piloted by God knows what sort of Arab or Turk or Mestizo. Fred came with me.

"I'll have that chocolate thing if you don't want it," he (Fred) said. "You actually *walk* home this time of night? What, you're impervious to the kind of people hereabouts?"

He was and is, Fred, an interesting example of a freelance cosmologist. It's now twenty years ago that he first showed how Uranus is the worst of the planets and then followed that up by positing the existence of "goldilocks" exoplanets orbiting "black widow" pulsars. I stopped under the next streetlamp, lifted my cuff, and exhibited to him the nine-millimeter Glock in my ankle holster. He marveled at it, slowly extracted the thing, fondled it, and then aimed it up at the streetlamp now hardly visible through a frenzy of lunatic insects. My weapon has a five-inch silencer, but I didn't want Fred trying it out at this time and place.

"*Five* incunabula?" he asked.

"Six."

"The devil you say."

"Sophocles. 1487. Aldine edition."

"Gold tooling, I suppose."

"Of course."

"Swine. I have a Baskerville. 1491."

"Sophocles?"

"Nay, nay. Polybius."

"Want to swap?"

"Amusing. I might let you look at it though."

"White of you. Could I have my gun back now?"

Instead, he aimed the weapon at a far-away police official and held it there. We were drawing nigher to one of the worse neighborhoods the city offers, a domain of substantial-looking buildings donated by tax payers to our less-evolved citizens. We passed on tiptoes. Aboriginal music exuded from the households, cars, and headsets. I descried a crime in process and one block further than that, a fire of appreciable size blazing in an intersection. Really, were it wise to have allowed these people to believe they're equal to us?

"No," said Fred, speaking in his authoritative style. "The theory of equality runs counter to evolution. Are we to believe that all Sapiens everywhere developed to the exact same station? Are all amoebas exactly equal? Tell me that after you've seen them at high resolution."

"No. I don't go that far."

"Rotifers? Paramecia? Horses?"

"I've seen some lovely horses."

We went on. My apartment occupies about one-fourth the second story of a dilapidated structure down on [address deleted] Street. Sheltered by the twenty-seven overhead apartments, neither rain nor snow nor lightning strike can injure my chameleons or book and Greek coin collections. Nor do I care if anyone mows the lawn or if the exterior needs painting. My apartment is quite good enough for a person of my kind and boasts a copper-reinforced door with a complicated lock and two simulated ones. Not even a nuclear attack—I long for it—could get me out of bed before nightfall. But I had started out to say that I purchased this apartment two years ago with one cash payment, leaving me entirely free of encumbrances apart from taxes, fees, insurance, requisitions, contributions, Halloween candy, and protection money. It was into this sanctuary of mine that I now allowed Fred to set foot.

"Gosh," he said. "I had expected something better."

"Yes. That's what people say about you."

"It lacks . . . I don't know. A woman's touch?"

"Get me one."

"And what's this painting, if that's what it is, hanging on your yellow wall?"

I served coffee. My table functions also as a chess board inasmuch as it displays the game's blueprint on its walnut surface. My friend had set down his coffee where his Queen ought to be.

"Your move," he said.

I desired to take my fine-tooth comb and use it on his appalling moustache. Coming back to reality, I courteously inquired, "Will you be contributing to our new magazine?"

"Oh, I suppose. But I'll need to see if it has the quality I want. The last time I submitted a piece, it was republished in some goddamned feminist journal coming out of Oregon for Christ's sakes."

"Sue. Sue them."

"Sure. And end up with a female judge? No, I'll tell you the squat truth-------------." (He used my name.) "We're not going to succeed with polite conversation. It's *weapons* we need. Serious ones. Explosives and so forth. Heavy duty. Big stuff!"

His face, already too chubby for his size and weight, was reddening. I sought to calm him by producing my Sophocles and allowing him to smell of it. This brave man had joined our group at the time of its formation and over the years had built a reputation among the readers of some of our best racialist journalists. Writing under the name *Theopompos,* everyone knew who he really was. But *Fred* was a pseudonym as well.

"I saw a jigaboo today," he said, "with a golden chain about his neck. However . . ." He paused to finish off his coffee. "Perhaps we really should have sympathy for this genus. Square pegs in round holes. How would *you* like it, to wake up in The Central African Republic?"

"Actually, I don't view it as a republic."

"Genetics is everything, and Jefferson was a fool. A smattering of genes is all it needs to distinguish grasshoppers from thee and me. It is said that but for a chromosome here and yon, men and women have the same DNA. And yet men and women seem quite dissimilar to me."

"Seems that way to me, too. My first wife for example..."

"Is it not ironic that America's very first dogma, equality, will be what kills us?"

I refreshed his coffee adding a tincture of brandy to the mix. He was getting sleepy while I for my part was impatient to get to my study and resume my nighttime schedule. Accordingly, I assisted him to the green room with its enormous bed and helped him with his shoes. That place has a particularly lovely wallpaper in which Smith's 1868 oil painting of the Battle of Leuctra is replicated in detail. A half-dozen books have been left on the window sill for the pleasure of my visitors, high-grade material that deserves to be used. But my guest was largely unconscious by now, and I had no difficulty retrieving my gun.

Four

In the days that followed, other members came to us bringing their women with them. We had rented the back room of the Pied Cow, a cozy restaurant with oak paneling and condign portraits on the wall. By this time, Taw had become more or less our bespoken spokesman, so to speak. He welcomed these new members with a brief talk and then one by one caused them to stand and tell about themselves. The women were shy, of course, save for a

youngish person, well-dressed and even good-looking albeit somewhat pale I ween was she. Recently divorced, her
aforetime husband insisted on dietary oddities and had
transferred to Israel.

But when it comes to action, we look to men. I was impressed by a certain chemist name of Henry (soon called
Hank by us) who had devised a wood-like product formed
from a heroin compound. Made into furniture and other
objects, he had been able to import large amounts of that
drug into American cities. (Later, I was to witness how he
"resolved" the stuff back into a dark white powder that
fetched high prices on the "black," if you know what I
mean, black market.) He vowed, and we believe him, to
bring the group at least fifty thousand a week. He also
possessed seven thousand acres of rich bottomland in
Missouri that I was proud to envy.

I slept that night between clean sheets but then awakened an hour later to secure my narrow window. It had
been raining and raining well to judge from things and yet
I had heard nothing on the roof situated at such a distance
from my books and lizards. A wind was up, and the tree
branches (there *are* some of these in New York City) were
slapping one anther frenziedly. I discerned a tiny dog
struggling uselessly against the wind. I then smoked a
brief cigarette and urinated into the rain.

I dreamt again, this time dreaming a dream that I were
in the South again. I thought I was swimming across a
profound blue lake in which the trout were multicolored
and could be viewed at a range of thirty feet or better.
There have been places like that though I couldn't cite
from memory the location or the moment I might have
been there. Came then to me pictures of my all-time favorite dog, a lumpy animal with a goofy smile. I then lifted
up my poor grey head, carried it to the other side of the
bed, and grabbed off another few hours of average-grade
sleep.

At seventeen minutes past the hour, I arose from bed and leapt to window to find the flood had also arisen and was lapping at the second story of the building just across the street. I marveled, my first erection in seven years egressing my paisley robe. A new diluvian age to curtail post-modernity? And were the grotesque structures of midtown Manhattan now drifting longitudinally toward Staten Island? The little dog at least was safe, having come to rest on someone's window sill. My mind fled back to Hesiod's remarks concerning the delights of the pre-urban stage. A world washed clean!

On the other hand, my electricity was dead. Just how on earth pray am I supposed to carry out my duties without lights and digital equipment? That was when I received a call from my dear friend Reece Rogers, a perdurable white supremacist with one of the country's loveliest wives. My cell phone was still functioning apparently, despite the climate.

"Reece baby! Are you loving this as much as I?"

"More. They say the water has blocked the Hudson Tunnel."

"Gorblimey!"

"Twenty-two inches in just seven hours. Sheepshead Bay is ruined."

"Oh, God. I pray it goes on for years and years."

"Yes, but that's not the main thing. The main thing is *sea water*. What you see now is absolute salt sea water bringing loads and loads of organisms of all sorts. Meantime, the niggers are looting everything, and the cops, the white ones, are shooting at 'em!"

His voice was restrained but I could see the ecstasy that underpinned his conversation. A dispositive racist of the eliminationist school, he was about five feet and nine inches in height and possessed degrees from some of the most lauded and most anti-white schools on the continent. His wife is just five foot three. Wife? No, these two people are simply cosignatories to a coital agreement and are continuing to copulate though they had voiced no wish for children.

"When are you coming over?" I asked, picking up where I had left off just above.

"How would I get there? Can't walk and can't drive."

"And bring your wife. Have her wear that green sweater. I'll fix spaghetti."

I could not, of course, prepare spaghetti in the absence of electricity, but I could however *read*. As mentioned, I do have an excelsior library that balances in quality what it may lack in extent. Running from floor to ceiling in two of my twelve rooms, the cabinets are of varnished walnut with transpositional shelving. Organized more with regard to aesthetics than subject matter, the books also serve as superadded décor and represent the chief benefit for having become rich. Or prosperous anyway. Fairly prosperous.

To accommodate the flood, I chose Blowinger's 1587 tome on the immediate Post-diluvian Age. Bound in leather, the volume is decorated with a discrete gold tooling and possesses marbled endpapers of good quality, an adventitious element no doubt. But far beyond all this were the little marginal drawings depicting capsized buildings, whales washed up on shore, ancient people racing for higher ground. Needless to say, the Latin was difficult for me, and soon I lapsed into studying the woodcuts only. I saw a comely woman clutching the gunnels of a drowning boat, her face the very image of hopeless despair.

Far too much time had passed by since our own country's last disaster. Reveling in the sound of water and rain, I returned to the window to find the road devoid of traffic apart from a recreational vessel moving slowly westward by means of an outboard motor. I retrieved my telescope, an inexpensive affair that magnifies only to perhaps three times real size, and trained it on the shopping center situated on higher ground where right away I descried the aforementioned negroes looting the stores. A burly man was making off with a white manikin whilst his children followed closely carrying what looked to be boxes of brand-new shoes. There came to me then a cellphone message that a "typhoon," she called it, had emerged last night from just offshore Jones Beach bringing 290 mph winds to New York City. This will not be the last such day for cities like this one.

They arrived by ferry, my friend and his woman, and managed to enter my building at the second-story level. She really had worn her green sweater though it wasn't precisely the edition I wanted. I gave them time to dry off and refurbish and be served with drinks, rather strong ones actually. From Reece, I learned that an enormous storm had broken out at the northern cusp of the Gulf Stream pushing 320 mph winds (and higher) into the coastal Northeast. Streams of traffic were striving (without full success) to exit some of the corridor's major cities.

"And what about the *West* Coast? San Francisco and all that?"

"No. Nothing happening over there," he said with feigned pretentiousness. "You can't have everything."

He had brought an essay for our prospective journal, a twenty-four-page disquisition neatly typed on pale brown paper. I took it and then retreated over to stage right where the light was better. No other light was available just then save what came from the enfeebled moon. The introductory paragraph, I must say, had been well-prepared and opened up a fresh perspective on the Jewish question. I wanted Taw to take a look at this. That man can take a piece of routine prose and make it glow.

"Wonderful!" I said. "This will go into our first issue."

The woman beamed, squeezing Reece's hand congratulatorily. Though not a conspicuous motion, it couldn't escape *my* notice. And in short, she was an admirable companion for an anti-Semite, and I would have enjoyed having three or four such people for my own wives.

"You claim that the 200 richest Jews dispose of two *trillion* dollars?" I asked her.

"At least that much. And that doesn't include mischlings. Why are you looking at my bosoms?"

"And what, pray, is the GDP of the Democratic Republic of Congo? For purpose of comparison I mean?"

"More debt that GDP."

"Ha. I think I see a solution here. Let the Jews give their two trillion to their blackamoor friends, and everything will be in balance once again."

"Sure, I'll let them."

We laughed, the woman, too. She had (has) a jolly smile, and her dentition is good. Further, her nipples appear to be blunt and of about the same dimensions of my original wife's—about half the length of your standard cigarette filter.

"How's she faring these days, your original wife?"

I had not expected this from the partner of my good friend. She knew enough about that marriage not to speak of it within my hearing.

"Don't you regret it sometimes, letting her slip away?"

"I had wanted to fix some of my special spaghetti for you but the electricity . . . I'm sure you'll understand. The electricity. And I don't have the right sauce."

"Don't want to talk about her?"

"Two trillion. Just think what we could do with that. Turn the *New York Times* into a suntan parlor."

"I had a letter from her just last week."

We adjourned to the next room. I do still maintain a standard billiards table there offering recreation to people deprived of electricity. But the light was poor, and instead of billiards my guests opted for another drink by candlelight. In the dim, their faces closely resembled those now serving as major tourist attractions on Easter Island. I was particularly reminded of the memorial to "Ferdy," a fugue-state personality positioned in such a way as to suggest he was looking up at the sky as his visage was being wrought in stone.

"I've been thinking about New Zealand," he said.

"Good."

"Beautiful place, the South Island especially. Over-whelmingly white. Very few Jews. Hardly any jigaboos at all." He drank.

"Yes, but what about all those Maori? God, they must be the most revulsive people on earth."

"That's a momentary problem. We can deal with them once we've established ourselves there. And the weather is divine."

I came closer. Reece had taken on a new appearance in the waning light and now bore the merciless aspect of a praying mantis. And then, too, he hadn't shaved in recent days which made it even worse. Devastated by admiration for her man, the woman was cuddled up next to him wearing a rapturous expression. And just when was the last time a woman looked at me that way? I shan't answer if you won't ask.

"Ten thousand well-heeled Aryan men and women. We could take over that whole apparatus in no time at all."

"Are you well-heeled?" I asked.

He pointed to his woman, the niece of a highly success-ful bond scammer. A decent-looking individual, she wore a silver badge displaying her genome and algorithm. "We don't have to have the whole outfit for goodness sakes," said she. "There's enough acreage on the South Island alone to domicile millions of high-quality white persons with nuclear arms."

She was mad and yet, the more she went on, the more excitedly I listened.

"Giant libraries. An opera house in every town. No advertising."

"First-class observatories to scan the Southern Sky. Maybe we could recruit Basil Falmouth to join us. He's doing interesting work on the psychological sources of the expanding universe theory. A hoax, he calls it."

We drank. Reece is perhaps the sixth or seventh most gifted anti-Semite in our group and ranks among the most prosperous. Heir to an auto parts manufacturer, he has lately begun vending interrogation equipment to certain anti-Zionist organizations in the Middle East. Shockingly—and I do *not* consider this as likely a successful venture—he has employed an epidemiologist and two bioengineers, one of them educated at Pskov University, to synthesize a contagious virus specific to Jews and mischlings. A humane strategy, it is not designed immediately to bring an end to these people but simply to sterilize those dwelling west of the Urals.

But now, daylight was drawing near. Mayhap we had drunk too much, and my friend had lapsed into a hypnogogic condition in which he was wearing a goofy-looking smile. The woman, too, was half-asleep and in the near darkness had become nearly as beautiful as my second wife. Where is she now, that wife, and does she ever rue having departed from me purely on account of my character?

I conducted my guests to the East Room and tried without success to assist the woman in preparing for bed. Space enough in that bed for three people though I didn't push the issue. It was after midnight when finally, I extinguished the candle, returning ten minutes later to find my colleague grinning insanely with figments of New Zealand running through his tortured head.

My own bed, broader than it needs to be, does give room for my pistol and pills and the two or three books I read rotationally as time allows. I adore sleep but seldom have more than five hours of it acquired intermittently with long intervals in between. I could read so much more quickly when I was young and my poor head not yet so cluttered with that amalgam of wisdom and rubbish that causes me to weigh more than I should. Tonight, I chose to pick up with Quintain's *Aujourd'hui et Autrefois*, a neglected classic too erudite for post-modern capacity. I adore the archaic prose, too, that tends to shut the door on weak minds. But hardly had I read five pages of that good stuff when I ricocheted over to Augustus Murray's *Iliad*, a better version than the original and the last best cure for people ensnared in awful times. Nor do I understand how last cures can fail to be best cures.

Five

They stayed with me the whole week, till business and digestive issues called them away. Myself, I eat in the standing position and never waste more time than necessary in the process. And then, too, we had encountered a slight disagreement over the tariff question, a matter of no real importance to either of us. I listened with declining patience as once again Reece began boasting unpersuasively of his cousin's role in facilitating the Rwandan Holocaust. The woman, of course, sought to turn the conversation to other things; wishing to reduce conflict, this gender, more attached to human beings than to ideas, always makes victory more and more difficult to achieve. We separated as good friends, however, and I have promised to take part in a certain "action" that even the *New York Times* won't be able to ignore.

The flood had receded, leaving behind a sampling of defunct sea creatures and urban detritus. On Tuesday, I ventured onto the street and moved gingerly down the glistening pavement to my preferred tavern, a tunnel-like establishment that exits on the far side of the city block. In contrast to my bright mood, the place was full of gloomy people slumped forward with their dewlaps resting on the bar. I know these types, mediocrities alarmed by a few starfish and yes, a few small octopi rotting on the walkway.

I had two drinks only and then sauntered down Pickens Street where a mob of people were lined up in front of a dry goods store. But even here, some of merchandise appeared to be moist. I then crossed over to Nathan Forrest Square and took the funicular up to the Stock Exchange where a great many little brown Jews were wailing in despair. Rising water had harmed the system, and styrofoam futures were down. I saluted a pair of teenage whores and then pursued my way down to the tip of Manhattan where a Staten Island Ferry boat had floated onto shore amid a waste of plastic bags and packaging material. A defunct fetus not much larger than a tennis ball was bobbing in the tide.

Never a more arrogant emblem, the world-famous Statue of Liberty was scanning the outer sea while nearer at hand a clutch of serious and very well-dressed businesspersons were debating market share, IPOs, and price-earnings ratios. A single Spartan youth could have slain the bunch of them with bare hands alone. Not to mention my own stalwart grandfather who had tamed the negroes of Coosa County with his admittedly-hefty walking stick.

Really, what manner of country is this after all? I strode past an advertisement picturing a purple dinosaur recommending a brand of toothpaste, girls in bikinis lauding a certain motor oil, a famous, I suppose, basketball player running for the Senate, his skull a perfect copy of certain recently-excavated types. I ventured on, passing a prune-face kike in Aryan clothing. A scandalous brothel staffed by she-males came up on the right with some score of unembarrassed old men pushing to get inside. By hap, I trod on a hypodermic needle, crushing that sucker flat. I came to an abrupt halt just then, aghast to discover the second son of my second wife lingering over a cup of assumed coffee just inside a cozy little café spilling over with artists and intellectuals dressed in pigtails and odd-looking spectacles. Wanted to vomit, I did.

He never saw me, however, and I was able to scamper past the window before then coming back to view the woman sitting across from him, a transracialized object with a shaven head. Her face, consequent to the violence of the patriarchy, appeared to have been used for driving nails.

I hurried past and proceeded on to Gretel's fifth-floor apartment where the Codreanu Society had conspired to meet. Never so foolish as to gather in the same place twice, I eschewed the elevator (it was damp) and climbed the eighty steps *one-by-one* up to where our host welcomed me with tea and wafers. She had put out a bowl of candies of various pastel colors, greens ones and so on, and as a patron of sweet things I hoisted a fistful of the things and began right away to use them.

Now this Gretel (not her real name) is the granddaughter of a heroic soldier burned to death by Bolsheviks just outside of Kursk. Her husband, too, had been "burned" by New York Bolsheviks who had destroyed his career over a legal issue manufactured by high-I.Q. Jews. Her hatred was as pure as twice-distilled water and powerful as the noise produced by the "Big Bang," improperly so-called. Really, I doubt there was any bang at all when sound didn't yet exist. Even Time itself, they say . . . But I digress.

It didn't exist either.

She is still a lovely woman, Gretel, endowed with rich breasts and a set of valentine-shaped lips that enhance the quality of her diction. I kissed her hand, lingering over it as long as allowed. The group had mostly gathered already, and such a group it was! I discerned Frank and his woman loitering over by the liquor and then a new member whom I recognized from the time I had helped to bail him out of jail. There were good brains in this room, including those that belonged to a Hellenistic historian with tenure from New York University. He would regale us sometimes with stories about that nest of Jews. And then there was Guillaume, an unreconstructed anti-Semite descended from the *Action Française*. We embraced in the French style, a somewhat discombobulating experience, and then ladled ourselves a helping of the good pink punch that did so much to promote the fanaticism of which we had need. I dawdled at a display of images that covered perhaps twelve square feet of space along one of the walls that formed ninety-degree angles with the walls attached to it. One drink and I needed to urinate. I delayed under a somewhat etherealized portrait of Dr. Goebbels and then padded on toward the toilet followed by Gretel's muddled dog, an aged creature who went about muttering to itself bitterly. Happily, our host had more than one toilet; else we old men would have had to use the window.

Not all of us were old, however, and I counted four, perhaps five individuals who looked able to hold their water for hours on end. Those were the days! I approached the Frenchman's woman, uttered a few words in that toneless language and then made an offer she charmingly declined. No, no, I only wished to say that as she doesn't smoke cigarettes, she wanted none of mine. I then pardoned myself and broached my friend Alois who was making progress, he swore, on our hoped-for journal. He was nervous in these rich surroundings and had the mostly bald head and ink-stained fingers of an underpaid law clerk in a Dickens novel.

"We're going to make you a rich man," I promised, "once you've got that journal in hand."

"I wouldn't mind being rich," he smiled. "How do you fellows do it?"

"Options. Arbitrage. Cattle futures. Why does anyone

work when it's so much nicer to let others do it for you?"

"And you can live with that?"

I thought before I answered.

"Barely. But we must learn from the Jews. They invented this stuff. And then, too, the price of rare books just keeps going higher."

"I see! And so how much—no, I'm just curious—how much do you pay, as it were, for those precious *objets* that you don't read?"

"Read 'em? Women don't crave rubies so's they can *eat* them. It's *beauty* we should be talking about!"

"I see. You're insane, of course."

"I understand that. I used to be normal, too, but life is so much more interesting this way."

We laughed merrily, or I did anyway. The other man's face had meantime taken on a look of significant disgust.

"How about all those poor people?"

"Look, my man, I've had lots of dealings with those people. You want beauty or justice? Can't have both."

He grinned feebly and then moved away. I liked him, however. It had begun to rain again and outside it was dark as night. A light drizzle tapped politely at the window panes. I adore this upside-down weather, so meet for a civilization now upside-down as well. I had neglected so far to visit the bathroom facilities. Just then, a trivial bird came to rest on the window sill but flew away when I came near. Some of the men had begun to draw off into the adjoining parlor where also Gretel and I went to join them. I had not realized that Taw was part of this get-together, and yet here he was, that long-fingered documentarian and gunsmith who writes pharmaceutical prescriptions upon request and large payments. He had shaved and dressed and in his large grey suit looked as dominant as he deserved to be. Respecting his anonymity, I shall not try to describe his appearance beyond mentioning that it corresponds to the likely preconception of those percipient people who have connections with others of the type as haven't we all? Today, it was a question of funding our effort to win control of a local television station, an almost impossible project in face of the Hebraic monopoly. Already that group has taken possession of at least forty percent of western tastes, misjudgments, and spending. My imagination turned back to Alexander who might so easily have put an end to this abomination all those years ago. Slay the Jew wherever you find him, Saint Louis had behested us.

I watched with admiration as Gretel took out her checkbook and made out a contribution of 100,000 dollars-worth of hard-earned money acquired by her forebears in 1943–44. He took the chit, Taw, savored it and then made the entry in his tidy ledger. But it will need millions more if we are to countervail against anti-white racism and the unappeasable lust for Jewish rule.

My good friend Hank (not his real name) gave $60,000 more. He had been doing well, more than just well by vending methamphetamine tablets to the derelicts in the city's eastern slums. Not that he sold the stuff himself! No, he was separated by three layers from the law officers and other vendors on his payroll. But how far oughtn't we go in defense of the culture given us by the Greeks? Better the whole world be addicted than to relinquish that.

"I'm getting interested in California," Hank revealed. "There's enough niggers over there to bring in fifty grand a month. And I haven't done *anything* about Chicago."

We praised him, some of us rising from our places to shake with him, bringing delight to his implausible face. Out in the drawing room, they were smoking and drinking and gossiping nonstop. Taw had himself given a fine sum—$75,000 I later learned—to help buy our local councilperson. I had no choice therefore but to take out my brokerage account and donate an amount commensurate with my standing. Followed then a brief film showing scenes from the conquest of France. We were toasting ourselves with waissels of mulled schnapps and the general mood was good. I finagled my way over to Gretel and again mooted that she come and move into my apartment but without receiving in return an invitation to take up in her more lavish domain. And so, at just after 5:20, I abandoned the place and went out into the rain.

New York City is not half so awful when it can't be seen. I traveled for perhaps an eighth-mile against wind and drizzle and then jumped into a novelty shop where umbrellas were on display. (I haven't hired a taxi cab in ages, not since I found myself late at night sitting elbow-to-elbow with some of the worst trash imaginable. I had about as soon visit a New York hostel with inter-racial trysts taking part on all sides.)

Back to the novelty shop: the clerk proved to be a white woman in her twenties I guessed, an astonishingly guiltless-looking person by the standards of the city. I melted, my heart reaching out to a woman who might possibly originate from my own part of the country.

"Mississippi?" I asked.

She grinned. "Baton Rouge! That's in Louisiana!"

I wanted to jump on her. She might have been as much as twenty-four or five, but never yet, lest I be sorely mistaken, had she passed a night in a hostel, she was that innocent. Divorces? Blow jobs? Cocaine? Not in a thousand years.

"I have a good-size apartment with lots of room," I said. "But just now, I'm in the market for an umbrella. The rain, you understand."

"I know! And it rained yesterday, too."

"Forty days and forty nights. You and me on an ark all our own?" (I didn't actually say that.) "Only Magellan could cope with this."

"Well sure; she's used to it by now. Anyway, we have lots and lots of umbrellas, and all colors, too. What color do you want?"

She emerged from behind the counter, permitting me to view her whole person. About five feet and four inches, she can't have weighed more than 119 pounds. When I was that height, I would have asked her out. Life is a lot more complicated than you people think.

"We used to go on long walks in the rain. No, no, not your fault. Anyway, she was a strange person. In some ways."

The wench had come up with a bright yellow umbrella, a veritable parasol bearing a floral print. I opened and closed the thing several times to postpone having to return to the rain. I then did exit and, eschewing motorized transport, returned and paid for the thing.

I wandered far, taking pleasure, some pleasure, in the haze and drizzle that fenced me off from the truths of that doomed city. Thirty feet below in the subway, rail carriages were shunting people back and forth. I know them—evil ones and good, all of them snared in an economic system. Myself, I don't see why we even need any stinking systems.

Okay I do, and in the next block I ran down into the subway and leapt aboard a car containing a crowd of the expected people. Some were sleeping. One man indeed seemed almost to be thinking though the bulk of them were "in neutral," so to speak. I discovered myself opposite a 300-pound negress with rectified hair and a green lipstick that really did sort rather well with her garters. Having evolved in a warm-weather climate too mild to require self-improvement, her thighs had fallen apart to reveal nothing that I, certainly, needed to see.

The next carriage was almost as full but offered a marginally better representation of the species. I trained my gaze on an overhead placard expressing esteem for a commodity having to do with a treatment for toenail fungus. Poor wretched human beings. I was filled with sympathy for them, yes and for reptiles, too. I am he who once viewed the photograph of a baby crocodile being squeezed by a boa of huge size. Our compassionate God! What a rotter that one turned out to be. He will bring that little crocodile to paradise?

But now I was myself being squeezed by a drunk who wanted to slumber in my lap. The next car was mostly free and by migrating on flaccid legs to the rear of it, I found a secluded place where I could philosophize over what I had seen this day.

The rain had slackened and by the time I came into my own neighborhood, I was able to fold my umbrella and follow a nervous-looking woman for two or three blocks until she began to run. Finally, I arrived home at 11:15 but only to meet a salesman posted in front of my apartment door. Four days earlier, I had clicked an advertisement for a certain product and here now was a representative of that company.

"No, no," I iterated, "I'm really not interested anymore."

"What did you say?"

"Not interested."

He grabbed my left arm, mistaking it I suppose for my weaker one. I managed to get inside however, quickly poured me a brandy and built a cheese and bacon sandwich. The television had come on of itself apparently and had returned to a retrospective football game from four seasons ago.

Six

I slept well and awoke unto a day whereof I knew not the date. My livestock appeared to have come undisturbed through the damp black night and my cuttlefish, acquired at some expense, were snoozing in the salt water tank maintained by my oceanography friend. I went then to my fraught kitchen and after putting coffee on the stove, hailed the half-dozen chameleons that shared my other aquarium, a seventeen-foot-long appliance kept always dry. I like to come close and look these creatures in the face. Their brains can't be greatly larger than a grain of rice, and yet they can forecast the stock market simply by changing shade. Good day for equities, less good for everything else.

Typically, I spend an hour or more each morning seated at my window. Historians come and go, but none has ever yet been able truly to delineate the actual look and feel of any past period. Your true historian, let's admit it, must be as devoid of morality as an entomologist. Myself, I have a clear impression of nineteenth-century France and the artists of that time, but I'm probably quite mistaken about the *texture* of actually having been there. Truth is, with only two or three exceptions, I can't remember being three years old. What is time? A transparent material, unreliable as smoke. No, I don't put a lot of credence in time, not after witnessing what it has done to so many old-time friends of mine.

Today, the cityscape was breathtaking, an excrementitious stain-on-the-world full of buildings with windows in them and sunbright bouncing off windshields. There was enough economic activity going on down there in just one day to sustain a normal civilization for a thousand years. What did they want really? Whatever it was, they wanted it hugely. I saw a tiny little man hurrying through the crowd to get to work on time. Bonds were up but endurables were down.

I made a quick call to Gretel who quite clearly was getting sick of me and then received a somewhat longer call from my second wife who desired tuition money for our sorry-ass grandchild. He had done well, or satisfactorily anyway in the Navy and now wished to study real estate at one of the state colleges. I am about as ready to subsidize that as to join the Anti-Defamation League.

"Oh, I don't know sweetheart. Maybe he should stay in the Navy."

"Air Force."

"And anyway, your husband can pay for it easily."

"Oh, God. He left four years ago! As well you know."

"And hasn't come back yet? The viper!"

I love that viper, a 24-karat dunce who absolved me of alimony. It was this that allowed me my books and cuttlefish and my 3,000 square-foot apartment with high-grade molding in almost every room.

I dined meagerly on milk products and a Tom Collins and then settled into my immaculate parlor maintained by that fussy old woman whom I pay so generously. The key to my desk drawer I keep in my wallet. Just because perfection is impossible out there in the world, that doesn't mean it can't be perfect up here on the fifth floor of a solidly-built apartment building offering a perspective of the encompassing slums. Next, I received a call from my good friend Lyle. I can't abide this person and have many times had to adjure his solution to the Jewish Problem which *cannot* be solved with brutality only. And now here he was once again, wheedling over the phone to visit me at home.

"Lyle baby!" I responded. "Getting any?"

"Can I come over? I got some . . . stuff to show you."

"Oh heck, and I was just fixing to go out."

"'Fixing?' You rednecks never change. Anyway, maybe I could come tonight?"

"No, no, come now. Please!"

He came over a half-hour later with a suitcase in each hand.

"Going to stay a while?" I asked. "Excellent, excellent."

He was dressed in shoes and a green gilet too small for his actual person. He has two eyes that seemed to belong to different persons, and his tatty beard had things living in it. He has a degree from Colgate but remains a cultivated man all the same, having made a name for himself in Anglo-Saxon grammar. Beloved by his students, he was currently living with his wife and a graduate student in a five-room apartment significantly smaller than mine. He has other qualities, too, some of them mentioned favorably in the staff directory of his upstate school.

"Lyle baby! Want to finish that chess match now?"

I fetched coffee for him and then dithered nervously with one of my digital devices while he opened the larger of the two valises, exposing a half-dozen disassembled Smith & Wesson M&P 15 Centerfire rifles with magazines variously holding between fourteen and twenty-six pieces of .223 ammunition. I marveled at this equipage. He seized up one of the weapons—his face had taken on a brutal expression—and aimed it at the sun.

"Bam, bam, bam!" he said. "How'd you like one of these hollow points going in one ear and out the other?"

"Not much. But better, don't you think, to start up a monthly magazine that might actually influence people?"

"Oh, I'll influence 'em alright!"

He was aiming now at one of my chameleons who had turned a terror-stricken red.

"Take ownership of a television station. Wouldn't that be better?"

"Pow!"

We talked at some length and then adjourned to the outside world and walked up and down the block for certain distances. It was here in one of the shop windows that I caught sight of my own or maybe his reflection. I had spent almost fifty years being young and never will be able to accept views of myself in my current incarnation. I tried to explain: "If we really want to free ourselves of the Jewish menace, intellectual weapons are much the best."

"Bam, pow! I can ream out a fifty-cent piece at seventy yards," he said aiming at one of the pedestrians.

The window across the road provided a reflection that I

hoped was *his*. I wanted to return, and did, to my apartment where yesterday another anti-Semite and his son had made themselves my guests in the upstairs room. These now descended quickly to take a look at Lyle. The boy, a tow-headed blond beast appropriated the rifle with the avidity of an Achilles.

"Bam!" he articulated, aiming the weapon at various appropriate locations in the putrefying city. "Pow!"

We grinned, three proud grownups pleased to see our instincts passing to the emerging generation. Just sixteen years old, the child had already won first place in his school's calculus competition.

"I got some grenades out in the car," Lyle confessed. "Shit, I can toss those babies up to forty yards on a clear day."

"Lyle, Lyle. But wouldn't it be better to own a newspaper, or senator, or a big television station of some kind?"

"Well, sure. But we can do more than just one thing at a time, can't we? My wife listens to music even while she's ironing. They have this little hickey you stick in your ear."

"Bam!" repeated the tow-headed boy. I'd have traded my third wife and two limbs for a child like that.

"Give you a million for him." (I didn't actually say this.) "Knows Greek does he?"

"Not yet. He's still on Latin."

"Bench press?"

"One hundred and fourteen percent of his own weight for Christ's sakes. What do you people expect actually?"

"Hundred and sixteen," the boy amended.

I brought out the forty-proof rum and prepared drinks, offering some to the child in a beaker that held two sizeable ice cubes also made of rum. My rum is appreciably more powerful than the ordinary kind.

There were now four certified anti-Semites in that room brought together just as spring was coming in and the little birdies who feast off the yeast I leave on the window sill were arriving more frequently. One, my favorite, is a disturbed individual with random eye beams. Getting down on all knees, a person could view the thing at close range through the double-glazed window. But do I digress? We anti-Semites are allowed to digress all over the place.

Seven

There still exists a supervised indoor shooting range at the corner of Ewell Street where one may use one's weapons without contravening the laws. I will sometimes visit that place along with my revolvers, my earplugs and ammunition, and today it seemed an ideal location for the entertainment of my visitors. The lanes are segregated by concrete walls, and only once, to my knowledge, has anyone been damaged by ricocheting slugs.

The place was already three-fourths full and with further niggers entering every minute. I did not feel in danger, however, not with my revolver and a ten-inch switchblade in my right sleeve. To administer a serious wound with a knife needs more pressure than readers might assume. In any case, they deemed me too old to bother with I suppose. Not that I claim to be an expert pistol shooter, not at all, but rather that I've had good success at disaggregating different sorts of fruits and vegetables with bullets in my soundproof basement. I nodded to the blackamoor in the next lane, identifiable by its egg-shaped head. He can run a hundred yards in ten seconds but can't rightly wipe himself I'll wager. We smiled at each other.

He expended his load all at once, leaving him at a huge disadvantage *vis-à-vis* myself. I took the opportunity to fire just three shots that however failed to alight precisely where I wanted. Were he that target, he'd still be breathing. I aimed and fired again, this time resolving the question rather more definitively.

Four lanes away, the sixteen-year-old Siegfried was handling one of the Glocks his father had brought back from North Carolina. Okay, he didn't yet have the aim we demand in members of our circle. I went to him, loaned him my earplugs, and instructed him about a number of things. His father was using an enormous weapon, a fifty-caliber (I believe) device capable of driving a half-pound load through a thousand immigrants standing in a row. The other fellow, Lyle so-called, had disappeared.

I left them soon after and then drove slowly to an undisclosed intersection at no great distance from my departure point. Except for intermittent clouds, the weather was bright enough to let me park my powerful red car just before a wire-hair jigaboo was able to preempt the space. I smiled. He was clothed in a dark blue suit that wouldn't have been inappropriate on a white man of good station. Did he believe that we could valorize the suit without noticing what was in it for Christ's sakes? Me, I left my fine automobile—not for another four hundred thousand years of slow-motion evolution would ever a negro be able to design a car like mine—and then strode across in front of him to reach the opposite shore. He was *not* happy with me, that much was clear.

This was the first of the people I was to examine at that intersection on that particular day. Moving like a man even older than me and with even fewer red brain cells, I occupied the conveniently-located bench where the usual thralls were waiting for the next bus to come along. A woman had taken up on the same bench, but I was quickly able to send her away by behaving strangely. Suddenly, I was assailed by one of those two-minute advertisements assigned electronically to the interior of one's eyelids, this one lauding a well-known law firm in Brooklyn staffed by ivy-league Yids. A bus moved past hurriedly, allowing me not nearly the time to evaluate the some two score of New York types on board. I witnessed a businessperson in new shoes marching past hastily to expand his company's market share. (You can memorize thousands of pages of Greek, Byzantine, and Persian history while reading not a word about market share. How wretched those people must have been.) I witnessed women in their thousands hungering desperately for what they couldn't name. My old grandmother, she expected very little but had no trouble naming it.

Came next the pathetic case of another down-and-out individual, a male, judging from him, who had spent his life catering to his social needs—a salary, office and title, insurance and voting permit. But wait, was I any different? Bet your ass I was and am! Had ever this person stayed up all night to finish a fine book? Or driven 240 miles into dark countryside despairing over a wife he had allowed to get away? I think not, no. No, there's just too much distance between me and the suits passing by. Moreover, this one possessed the sort of nose I just cannot endure, a stubby affair with two flared nostrils sucking at the New York air.

Yes, I need to get me back down South again. But the next vision was somewhat better—a twelve or thirteen-year-old churl who might almost have been southern, too. Still young enough to be baffled by a number of things, he was gaping at some of the very same pedestrians referenced above. We looked at each other, we brave Teuto-Celtic men, but then both quickly looked away again.

"Hey there!" I wanted to shout. "How's the fishing today?"

"Fair to middling," he would definitely have said. "They was hitting wurms pretty good till all these Yankees scared 'em away."

"Dagnab it! I ought to of gone with you."

He faded into the business-class crowd carrying his harmonica with him. And yet, I could predict a reconstructed career for him as a well-dressed big-city arbitrageur adept in currency futures. Is this now what life is for? *My* son, supposing I had had a good one, would be rehearsing guerilla warfare down in Bibb County.

The next person was a middle-age woman whose husband had been slain, as I imagined, in one of our country's efforts to bring free market democracy to those districts where it was most in demand. She was tired, old, thickening about the middle, and her offspring were far less interested in her than in the new anal intercourse procedure going around. She walked slowly, her shoes were brown and had perhaps belonged to her husband at one time. I didn't say anything, however.

Needing to urinate, I returned hastily to my car. Apart from two speeding tickets and a small matter having to do with 1998, my police record was not just clean but abnormally so and, as explained previously, I never want again to be interviewed by a Yankee police officer with up-to-date interrogation equipment. Accordingly, I retrieved that empty mayonnaise jar stored beneath the seat and while maintaining a self-righteous expression filled it with 98.2-degree urine. But for only a very tiny protozoan running about on the bottom, the fluid was clear and of good color. I was easily able to empty the container into the sewer and then witness in the rear-view mirror as the rivulet sped off for perhaps fifteen rods before being absorbed in the pores, as I supposed, of the concrete itself.

I had been listening to a quite good performance of the violin concerto of Sibelius, but now that was coming to an end. It was while I was considering what next to play that I perceived a negro in modern disguise sauntering down the avenue in such a way as to suggest that it might have been *his* ancestors instead of mine that had split protons and conquered North America. I grabbed up my binoculars and trained on his suit and clothes, a better ensemble than anything presently standing at attention in my own closet. These people, they may confound millions but I know all about that genome that reveals itself in action. Fumbling awkwardly with the half-dozen devices on my dashboard, I focused my QCA (Qualified Cognition Approximator) on the rear of the negro's head and tried in vain to locate the sweet spot just above his right ear. This amazing invention had proven almost perfect in identifying a person's aggregate intelligence even if I have so far demurred using it on myself. But just then something to be described in the next paragraph jumped to my attention and caused me to put the implement aside.

My second wife, or anyway someone who resembled her to within an ace of the original, emerged just that moment from the department store and began to stride off efficiently with a purchase in a plastic bag—a smock or underwear or likely a pair of matched shoes with a tiny jar of polish included free of charge. She was happy—I know these people—and moved forward as breezily as if she were twenty instead of the seventy-four I computed her now to be. I followed her, of course, but had to exert myself in the process. Even today, she was still thirty-four months younger than me. I called twice, using the pet name I'd assigned to her in '85, but I shouldn't have been surprised when she opted not to answer. In any case, my second wife had looked not at all like this person.

I saw other wives over the next half-hour, including one who looked so much like my third wife's sister that I waited for the chance to run over her with my fine vehicle. In the meantime, the Sibelius piece was coming down to the best part, and I was unwilling to exit so soon my parking space.

Eight

I slept decently well over the next three days and nights but then was awoken much too early by those routine street noises that in this place serve in lieu of roosters.

New York is a containment pen for befuddled people who talk to pigeons. Me, I can see through walls and know only-too-well what New Yorkers do. Taking up my inexpensive telescope, the one harbored in the top drawer of my bedside table, I closed in upon the apartment complex across the avenue where a retired man in an undershirt sat watching a basketball game on daytime television. Like most organisms, we may assume that he wants to go on living, but why? When was the last time he had an experience that ranked higher than a two or three on my personal ten-scale?

I sought to get a view of the man's quarters but was able to bring only very little of it into focus. He had a bowling ball, the imbecile, on the mantel piece and next to that a standup photo—and here I had to dither with the scope for a more legible view—standup photo of his purported wife, a barnyard exemplar with an indignant face resting on 230 to 250 pounds. And she, too, did this one also wish to go on living and voting her conscience to make things better in America? Suddenly, that instant, the actual woman herself hove into view with a cup of coffee and tiny dog and proceeded to situate herself on the sofa just next to her lout of a husband.

No, this is how it is in America where the most delicate political and social decisions rest upon the choice of human beings. Better to consult a pair of dice. I then turned my gaze two windows over and three down where a gaunt-looking man was scanning my own building with a telescope of his own. Immediately, I left off what I was doing, adjourned to the library, and victualed my lizards with an eye dropper. They do seem to have a certain affection for me, and I'm not so lofty as to refuse it. Named after certain personalities in Homer, I keep them separated behind glass walls.

To be truthful about it, it was January now, and apart from an illustrated edition of Ho Chen's great classic, I hadn't received the first Christmas present as yet. Oh yes, I do have colleagues and coadjutors, but at my age it's the worst kind of folly to nostalgicize about those pre-post-modern times when people seemed actually to be interested in each other, as we then believed. Me, I could perish right now and still have to wait two weeks before the Jews discovered my stocks, bonds, and dinnerware.

I dislike receiving mail which has to be burned and shredded. I could contribute, say, a few hundred dollars to some of the more worthy ones or give a really significant gift to the best of them, in this case a plea on behalf of an imprisoned white man accused of murdering an interracial couple caught walking together openly in the streets of Long Island City. In the event, I wrote a check for one thousand and sealed it with a kiss.

The last and best of the mail included a letter from one of my dearest and most admired colleagues, an educated tri-lingual author from Florida named *Rodney Quartz* (not his real pseudonym). This remarkable individual along with five, perhaps six white colleagues had set up a forty-acre breeding farm in the interior of panhandle Florida for the production of transplantable organs needed by a certain Jewish medical center (not named here) in New York City. Extracted from the local population of incarcerated negroes, these glands and other tissues could sometimes fetch half-a-million dollars from pecunious consumers needing transposed kidneys, lungs, pancreases, and the sort. Some Jews indeed accept negroid hearts without asking the actual source.

To increase his stock, Rodney would occasionally cover some of the comelier black females himself, producing a light-hued and more intelligent yield for upper-caste Middle Easterners in need of breeders and catamites. This was the Rodney, the very one whom now I went forward to greet at the former *Idlewild Airport.*

The traffic was not good, and meantime I was en-

gulphed with telephone messages arriving from all parts
of the world. I can predict that less than 2% of those calls
should be acknowledged, and yet I have sometimes been
given information and alerts in the absence of which I
could not have survived. And then, too, Bruckner's Ninth
Symphony was playing on the machine, and someone, a
jigaboo of some description, had rolled down his window
and was screaming at me from the other lane. Up ahead, a
worn-out little car had brushed up against a great one
causing the great driver to leap from his cockpit. I often
see this pattern in New York City. I wanted to stay for it,
but the car just behind me was pushing forward with what
looked to be a bumper with barbs on it. Life is dangerous
in this most prosperous city in the world. I caught a pe-
ripheral sighting of an unambiguous slut half-asleep in the
rear seat of a vehicle traveling in parallel with me. From
above, a helicopter was offering a weather caution to the
drivers. Snow was expected. A dead animal lay off to the
side, its belly broken open to reveal the inner workings of
your ordinary cat. Suddenly, apropos of nothing, the radio
came on presenting an in-depth interview with a famous
hockey player. Long ago and far away, things had not always been like this.

I came to the airport without mishap and found a parking niche between two Asian-made cars. Having no lug-
gage apart from my revolver, I was able to wend my way
among the black and brown travelers loitering in the ter-
minal. I am not an especially large person, but most people do tend to get out of my way once they catch sight of
my facial expressions. Stopping neither for coffee or cigarettes, I proceeded to the *Magic Carpet Airways* and
formed up in line behind a harried woman with two non-
Aryan children. For the life of me, I could not recall having summoned these people to enter my once-beautiful
country. These children, a boy and something else, had
obviously been trained to believe there was nothing wrong

with them.

The clerk turned out to be an especially friendly person—should I have asked for a date?—and never mind her tribal scars. As an open-minded, tolerant, and extroverted sort of type, I smiled right back at her. The best place for my blade would have been that two-square-inch patch just above her unimpressive left breast. White people? I spied perhaps two dozen in that whole enormous space.

Now I had not myself ever viewed this "Rodney" face-to-face. I foresaw him as a tall individual, distinctly white, with an intelligent forehead, a dark blue suit, and congruent tie. I hurried to what I supposed to be him and tried to relieve him of his suitcase whereupon he spun about to face me.

"Nothing of any real value in there!"

"Ah."

"Just some clothes and business papers. You'd be bored."

I left him. No doubt the actual Rodney was at the back of the line mixed with that giggling throng of Mestizo girls under guard of a large Mexican type with a mustache and oily hair. Time was passing, I was getting older and hadn't had a smoke in thirty minutes. In the event, it was Rodney who discovered *me*.

"-------------?" (He used my name.)

I acknowledged it and shook enthusiastically with him. He seemed to be an acceptable human being who stood out conspicuously from the crowd. He appeared to me notably younger than his supposed seventy-seven years, due possibly to the injections he was gossiped to have endured. I conducted him straightway to the airport bar situated about sixty rods from the place where we had been searching each other's eyes for the underlying integrity assumed to be there. A fascinating individual, he had already published two volumes of original poetry in Cherokee. His English, however, was weak and vitiated with an almost impenetrable accent.

"A good flight?" I asked perfunctorily. "That man over by the water fountain seems to be watching us."

"Right. He spotted me in Atlanta and has been following me for three days."

"CIA?"

"Possibly. Or maybe he's still trying to sell me that property in the Bahamas." (I am transcribing his speech in a much more understandable version than what actually came from his lips and teeth.)

We hastened to order drinks but had to wait for the bartender woman, a chocolaty lady with a beauty spot next to her nose, to fetch us the beverages we had chosen. Rodney's drink had a cherry in it which, however, disappeared in the immediate aftermath of his very first quaff.

"You should be pleased, ------------," he tried to say, "with the money I've brought you. Another year and we'll have enough for that magazine."

"Television network."

"That, too. And a couple dozen cannisters of that new stuff."

We drank. The new stuff can be *aero-dispersed* by means of drones while leaving no residues in human tissue or tell-tale fragrances in the air. Came then the news over television of an unexpected increase in the balance of trade deficit for this month. I turned suddenly on the man following us but was not able with my gaze alone to send him on his way. In my jacket pocket, I had half a dozen tranquilizers where I could get at them quickly. The largest, which I now seized up and tossed down with a swig of rum, was an innocent-looking affair of commensurate dimension. Of a pinkish color, the pill acuminated to a point at one end but remained as flat as possible at the other. I waited for the calming effect, a "weather condition," as it seemed, that let me unravel my taut fists and take no more heed of the pullulating foreigners In all sides. Rodney took two.

"So!" I said. "And how *is* business these days? Generally speaking." (I hadn't wanted to broach the subject earlier. The place had hundreds of ears moving in and out and loitering all about.)

He came near, whispering in my better ear:

"Wonderful. We can now take out twenty-four inches of small intestine and preserve it for six days in frozen formaldehyde."

"Six!"

"Ssssh! Quiet."

"And so we can sell the stuff in Europe now?"

"Or sell it back to the jigaboos themselves."

Impossible to keep from laughing.

Nine

I dreamt that night that my little fifty-acre patch in Alabama had come under siege by the people I'd seen at the airport. It was 3:02 when finally I adjourned to the toilet and then to the kitchen for a glass of milk. Another racist (I recognized him) was having a bowl of cereal while scanning the second-most awful newspaper in New York City. We nodded to each other, and by the time I had returned to my own room, the rain had come back again. Recovering my dream after a short effort, I then altered the plot to bring my former wife together in bed with me.

I found in the morning that it had been a significant rain even if not approaching that downpour of three weeks ago. There were no traces of salt brine on the pavement, and the sea had not overflowed the city on this occasion. It will need a perfect concatenation of rain and polar ice melt I suppose, before the city may consummate its fate at last.

I detected no sound from my guest and seized the opportunity to take up my position at the window with a cup of coffee whilst watching New Yorkers padding off to their office buildings. I simply cannot fathom why people dress up in church-going clothes in order to squander away their lives carrying out the demands of their inferiors. No one I admire ever allowed himself to be treated like that. No, it's more honorable in my opinion to be a risk-taking criminal than to dither away more than, say, three or four hours a week in commercial activity. That's what I say to young people—that it's better to be a risk-taking criminal, etc., etc. A quick death is better than a protracted one. That's what I say to those people.

"Oh?" said Rodney. (He had come up from the basement.) "If it weren't for commercial activity, how would we have over ninety-seven million in the bank?"

"By thieving!" I replied wittily. "Tell me, do you even pay those poor wretches when you lift out their glands?"

"They don't feel a thing."

"That wasn't the question."

"Oh, for goodness sakes. Why do they need money when they're going to be dead?"

I couldn't logically answer.

We had coffee and then two each of those little pastel-colored, pink and yellow *petits fours* to which I am so partial. We had a full day's work in front of us, but I wasn't willing to quit my cozy home till the crowd had thinned and the underwriters, statisticians, and government bees were in their work stations doing normative things. I excused myself long enough to repair to the blue room where my neglected computer was spilling over with dozens of uncalled-for threats from some of our enemies. Our truly dangerous enemies would never be so foolish. There must also have been a hundred messages promoting therapies unavailable elsewhere—tonics to stimulate hair growth, DIY transgendering kits, truth syrups, erectile pulsars, and video tapes for all sorts of tastes. With this technology, one can learn more about the American people than from all the census reports combined. And someday, I know, the human race will give up on itself and file quietly away without complaint.

At 9:48, we spilled out into the still-moist weather and hiked uphill to where the funicular carried us to the East Aloe subway station. There were some individuals loitering on the platform but as always I had my Smith & Wesson with me. I noted one particularly suspicious person, though I couldn't, of course, know exactly what he was suspicious of. His arms hung down on both sides, and he wore a hat that seemed to contain more than just a head.

"Look at that one," Rodney whispered.

He motioned toward a largish African American Jigaboo dressed in a simulacrum of a standard business suit, a healthy-looking person in spite of his evolutionary arrearage.

"Impressive."

"Pancreas, gallbladder, cecum, the whole ball of wax. Take it apart, you got yourself another million for our investment account."

"I'm thinking real estate these days. REITS perhaps."

We moved on, pioneering our way amid clusters of Chinese, Chinese-Americans, American Chinese, and other homologous material. Am I the last to remember when America was a more or less white country with European characteristics? I wanted to cry.

"Careful!" said Rodney, taking my elbow and guiding me around a clot of far-too-dark people completely inapposite for America.

"No," he said. "We're the inapposite ones now."

I tried not to look at them, coveys of aliens feasting on the remains of a once-promising civilization. A costume ball, a genetic joke, triumph of excrement over gold. Too late to look away, I was offered the sight of a 375-pound negress moving toward me, a man-o-war leaking on the sidewalk. In a place like this, a standard white person often needs to look skyward and hide his face, as the poet said, amid a crowd of low-hanging stars.

We continued, the story of my life. I knew so little of Rodney's life and accomplishments, save only that there had been many of them.

"I believe, like me, you've been married more than once yourself, right?" mooted I. "Anyway, that's what Reece said he had been made to understand from a friend of one of Taw's people."

We moved on. My friend was still carrying that worn-out brown-leather satchel that was beginning to weigh on him. It must have weighed considerable and had a moist stain on it. I moved to the other side of the man and took out an electronic cigarette. Adults are allowed just one of these a day in New York City who must alert the Department of Health and Human Services half an hour in advance. The tobacco, or electrons, rather were very welcome on this blustery day and empowered me to turn my mind away from the city and its things.

"Three wives." said Rodney, accepting a cigarette and lighting it from mine. "But one of them died."

"Died!"

"Disappeared in a car crash."

"That's rotten, just rotten. But how do you rank her as compared, for example, with your other wives?"

We had come to the designated building, a limestone pile with a compassionate inscription running around the architrave. We climbed the steps and entered an impressive lobby displaying an optimum map of Israel and a bronze tablet listing the names of contributors in order of dollar amount.

"No comparison," Rodney whispered. "The first one was sacrosanct, the others pure shit."

I experienced a significant increase in my feeling of kinship with this aboveboard colleague of mine. We entered and seconded ourselves to the fourth floor by way of the elevator and then exited into an opaline hallway full of short, dark, bearded-looking people moving past hurriedly with knitted eyebrows that joined above the nose.

"Hebrews," I explained to Rodney.

Our appointment was for room number 101 wherefore we went there right away. Six persons sat in the waiting area, these, too, very like those moving past in the hall outside. The Jewish genome, I've been told, hasn't perceptibly changed since the days of Ur. We were ushered through the operating room—no need to tell about that—and then into the maternity ward crowded with Jewish material squalling at high volume. And came at last into the fetid-smelling office of the CFO himself. No need to speak of this either, except to say there's no need to go into it apart from reporting that he was short, dark, and his fingers had been largely eaten away by too much exposure to X-ray beams, as I supposed. He had seen me watching his hands.

"What, you think I did this on purpose? Chewing off my fingers? Hey! I got fifteen putzes here for that. What, you want I should go home with blood on my feet?"

"No, of course not. No, we just . . ."

"Black niggers following me home? What am I, a play-goy who don't know who's on first?"

"No, no, Abe; of course not. But just look ahere at what we got for you!"

As the husband of his first wife, Rodney then tried to settle the satchel on the CFO's kidney-shaped desk, which is to say until the kike required him to relocate it to the floor. We gathered around, we three, joined by an anti-Aryan woman with a bitter mien. Rodney, or "Rod," as we sometimes called him for reasons to be explained later on, had already taken a pair of gloves from his jacket and after some problem had rigged them up on the befitting hands. ("Rod," we called him, because it seemed best to do so.)

"First, I'm going to let you see one of the sweetest little

bladders this side of the Chesapeake," Rodney said. "Mint-new, this sucker. Took it off a nigger not thirty-six hours ago."

The interior of the package was splashed with blood but the organ itself was visible enough. It weighed, I imagined, about two pounds only and yet was priced higher per gram-unit than the best cocaine. The Jew examined it from every angle, confessing finally: "Not bad, not bad. Okay, give you two hundred for it."

"Jesus," uttered Rodney, "H. Christ! Knew it! I just knew you'd try to Jew us down!"

"Maybe he can't help it," I contributed.

"Two hundred? It ain't worth two hundred thousand to save a kike?"

He put the organ back, did Rodney, and then very delicately and using both hands scooped up a much larger piece of merchandise of about the size of something three-fourths as small.

"Tell me, how do you like the looks of *this*?"

"Not bad. What can I say? Hey! You want I should get down on my knees?"

"Seven hundred and fifty. You can't do better than that. Nobody can."

"Can't nobody do better, he says. Hey! Maybe I should get in touch with my cousin Moise. He lives in Flatbush."

"He wants to buy it?"

"Sure! He'll eat anything. If it's kosher."

"Okay, just hold it right there!" (I could feel my gorge acting up.) "You should know that his patience, Rodney's, and mine, too, is *not* unlimited! *Are not*, I mean."

"So? You should see *Moise's* patience! He don't got none."

My forbearance at its all-tine low, I unholstered my Smith & Wesson and showed it to him.

"Bad," the Jew said, putting on his glasses and looking at it. "What am I, some little *noodge* you can do this to?

You don't even know how to use that thing!"

"He might," Rodney said. "He has a background in Alabama."

Slowly and with delicacy, the surgeon pulled open his drawer. He had a weapon of his own in there but opted not to use it at this time. What sort of weapon was it that I saw in there? I will say that he had a variety of medications stored in little brown jars that looked as if their contents were equally the same. Cautiously, Rodney, or "Rod," took up one of the bottles and after decoding the label, pried off the little white plastic cap and consumed two oblong pills of greenish hue. He then sent the nurse for water and turned back to the CFO who sat scratching his wattle with that selfsame ballpoint pen used for writing prescriptions and now this $500,000 check. Rodney gave it back to him.

"No checks," said Rodney. "We require six hundred now, for all the trouble you've caused."

"We don't have that much!"

"Okay, let's make it seven hundred then. Plus, ten percent for me and five for the man with the gun."

Very slowly, he drew out his purse. A large total, eight hundred and five thousand in paper bills suffocating in the portraits of psychotic northern generals; the whole mess must have weighed twenty pounds. We shook all around, this, too, done ungraciously I thought. Out in the hall, I spied a feeble man limping hurriedly to the operating room, impatient, as I imagined, for his new organ. We departed quickly, Rodney and myself, took the elevator to ground zero and strolled toward Fifth Avenue.

"Are they following us?"

"Of course not. There're far more of us, and they can't bear to lose even just one of them to a faulty bladder. Hell, they'd harvest every spare part in the world if they could." And then, after a short pause: "Besides, those organs are all diseased, most of 'em, and won't last a year. Jews aren't the only ones who know how to think like Jews."

Ten

Pleased to be shut of him, I left Rodney at the subway and then turned toward home taking the money with me. Though I'm not officially the treasurer of our group, it often happens that our funds pass through me in the partly-true belief that I know how best to invest them. And, too, I have a good relationship with one of the officials of a certain New York bank (not named here) who for a token fee allows me to deposit large sums without having to answer questions. Nor was I loath to put the $35,000 in my own small account.

The day was turning dark, and I had miles to go before I planned to stop. The traffic was awful even by local standards, and the depleted office workers were keen to return to their abodes where some of them (but by no means all) had cheery wives in aprons waiting in the doorway to welcome home wage-earners broaching every day a little nearer to the grave. Really, were it not better to lie among the already-dead who fell at Adrianople on that dread day?

I prepared a drink and was about to settle on the sofa when I collided into a guest I had forgotten about. One of my ice cubes had dropped into his cuff and we bumped heads trying to dig it out.

"Ah!" I said. "My fault."

"Yes."

Another racist was in the dark part of the room striving to read the New York telephone directory (the "bestiary," he called it) in insufficient light. Had they been meeting here in my absence, Frank, Fred, Alois, and finally Gretel, the last to step into ken? I had been looking forward to a quiet time, an alcoholic drink, a few pages of Cockayne's *Leechdoms, Wortcunning, and Starcraft*, all to be followed by six to eight hours between taut sheets; instead, I had now to rouse myself and offer treats to the gathering, specifically cake and ice cream and a few other analogous materials of the sort that we were wont to offer one another when we must. Only Gretel actually lauded my poor festive efforts, and Gretel is a woman. Came now the moment to describe my activities of that day. I stood and coughed twice and then somewhat timidly began my story:

"Well, it was really something," I said. "Old Rodney and me, we . . ."

"Good, good. But how much did you get? Was it more than last time or was it, like, less? Was it several hundred thousand, or just a few simple thousand net? And what did you get for that great big old lung?"

Reece held up his hand. He had been standing in the kitchen doorway where I hadn't noticed him up until this time.

"Big old lung? Big old lung? I thought we offered *quality*, size notwithstanding."

"We do!" I riposted immediately. "We all know about that fighter who won the Middle Weight Championship, yes? A whole year went by before they found out he had cancer."

"That's nice. But coming back to the subject at hand, how much did you get for the goddamn thing?"

Gretel then extinguished her cigarette, causing the thing to sink up to its elbows in her unsampled ice cream.

"Was it a million, or more than that? Or was it *five* million or a great deal less than that?"

"It was," I stated plainly, "less than that."

A groan went up. A tall man, never seen by me before, stood, got into his coat, and abandoned the room in annoyance. I began to understand that these people had been strategizing in my absence and had expected a larger return on the organs. And it is true that seven hundred

thousand is not such an impressive amount when meas-
ured against the overhead, the salaries, rent, corpses,
equipment, and so forth that had been needed to produce
it. Despite my advice that English majors could do the ex-
tractions, Rodney had employed at stiff cost actual medical students from a school in Costa Rica. More importantly, we needed to identify a better class of recipients, billionaires for example and State Department officials with
access to offshore funding.

"Imagine," said I speaking to the group at large, "imagine the official in charge of foreign aid to Israel, imagine
he got sick. Imagine he needs a heart. Are you following
me? How much would they not pay, those people, to keep
the money flowing?"

"Lots." someone shouted out.

"Lots? They'd pay a hell of a lot more than that!"

"But would they," asked I, "produce an anti-Communist
film in Hollywood?"

I had gone too far. To get back to reality, I asked how
we might better identify a more frightened grade of Jews
in need of transplants. Or better, how to increase the
number of such people. There was no question but that
we were finally beginning to close in upon a solution to
the Jewish question. Why shouldn't a half-billion dollars
in the hands of trained racists prove able to salvage the
West? Because it's too late already? I thought of those
iron-willed Confederate soldiers willing to die for just one
chance at a blue-belly northern abolitionist.

We debated till midnight and a little past whereon the
guests began to leave. I caught up with Gretel who
claimed she couldn't stay. Her eyes were rotten with lust,
and I was enflamed by the nudity of her arms. I noted Taw
still loitering palely in the library, a fat volume splayed
open in both hands. I went to him. It needed half a minute for his eyes to adjust to me, an aftereffect of the years
he had spent squinting at fine print. Had ever anyone

produced so many illegal documentations or plausible bills of currency? I showed him the vellum shoes ($800) I'd bought with one of his fictional documents. We often used these, the membership, for small purchases, and it was rare that I carried less than two or three thousand dollars-worth of such stuff in my scuffed wallet. We shook solemnly in the membership's style.

"Taw! How long have you been here?" I asked.

"Since Tuesday. But the bedrooms were already full."

I smote myself on my own forehead. I could easily have made room for him in the furnished attic, a civilized area full of books and other cultural equipment.

"My goodness, Taw! I could easily have made room . . ."

"No, no, I like it here. That red leather couch."

"Yes, I've done more reading on that item than in any bedroom in the house."

"*Cow* leather, is it?"

"I think so, yes. The artificial stuff wouldn't smell like that."

"I dare say."

We sat on the red cow sofa. The man had prepared an American birth certificate for an anti-Semite domiciled in Austria and entrusted me to pass it on to him. The falsification, as always, was splendid and included a set of reasonable-looking footprints of proper size. He then pulled a few hundred-dollar bills from his portmanteau which I declined. Too prudent to produce bills of larger denomination, he was content to keep our more threadbare members in reliable pocket money.

"Life isn't fit for you Taw," I suggested. "Life is for shallow people."

"Yes, but if we can get organized, we cognizant types..."

"We'd still be outnumbered a thousand to one."

"No doubt. But some people are worth *more* than a thousand of the other kind."

"Thanks," I said, blushing.

I served drinks. He had gone back to reading, or any-way striving to read in my 200-year-old copy of Podgor-ney. The book was fatigued, and the hinges under duress, which might explain why he held it in his lap in that par-ticular fashion. If I haven't already said so, his eyesight is worthless, and it remained a mystery to everyone that he could navigate the city and do what he did in regard to documents and business papers. He launched into the Jewish Question:

"If only we'd known," he started out, "that they had in-tended to change our Aryan nation into a Jewish one. They'd never been allowed to dock their ships!"

"Naïveté. How strange that our 3,600-year-old civiliza-tion should end this way."

"Absolute, universal, categorical, dispositive equality all the way down, the nightmare philosophy. Equality fueled by billionaires. Why aren't you laughing?"

"Yes, but you have to admit that they know so much better than other people how other people ought to be-have."

"Lenin, Moses, and Bolshevism."

"And all that indignation!"

"Could have been worse. Imagine there hadn't been the holocaust."

"And how long O God before another?"

"I know a nicer solution."

"Love to hear it."

"Terraform an exoplanet. No, some of the fellows are already working on this. Terraform a good-size planet in a strange location far away. No, actually this could be done in just a couple thousand years they say. Okay? Terraform that baby and transport all the good people there."

"*Two thousand years?* We'll be dead by then!"

"Ah! And so you view yourself as one of the good peo-ple then?"

I looked down. Truth was, I really had sometimes

thought of myself that way. I could hear him still speaking when I was in the kitchen mixing drinks.

"They just can't endure it," he testified. "Our Aryan societies are so antithetical to their racial nature! For them, I suppose, it's like living in a horror house arranged for Halloween. After all, it needs only two or three genes to cause the races to dread each other."

"Half a dozen maybe," I amended.

"Or consider your standard negro for Christ's sakes. I'm surprised we can even talk to each other."

"We can't."

We were interrupted by an urgent call offering a ten percent discount on four table settings of dinnerware made in Pakistan, a shockingly persistent offering that had followed me from machine to machine for seven years. The gadget indicated I had 227 other calls waiting for attention, but I preferred to deal with my guest.

"They say that they believe"—he snorted—"that they are equal to us and crave to take revenge on us for knowing that they ain't. They wish to squirt as many gallons as possible of seminal toxins into our ladyfolk while allowing us to fight their wars for them."

"And the remedy?" I asked, watching closely for the answer.

"Extermination, plain and simple. And *all the way down*."

We stood, shook, and drained our glasses dry.

And dreamt that night that my second wife had come back to me, except there were three of her now. Dressed in heels and bright red skirts, they stood about in various places, some of them humming at the stove, some dusting the furniture, some sorting through my opera recordings, and some—there were more than three—preparing coffee or seated at that old vanity dresser combing out their hair. My idea of paradise, ladies and gentlemen. But it couldn't last, of course, not with Taw walking up and down in the

library speaking words I couldn't interpret. And now so
soon after the Solstice, ended thus the day.

I am usually penalized for pleasant dreams and after
perhaps an hour of medium-quality sleep, I began to visualize human faces drawing near, some of them so detailed
and convincing that I knew they had actually existed at
one time. An old woman I saw, medieval in appearance,
my own mother's ancestor she looked to me. A man hoe-
ing weeds. I sense them all the time, looking down on me
from their positions in the sky.

I collected perhaps five hours sleep that night, arising
finally at just after 4:17. The night was as dark as winter
nights in Queens are wont to be. My chameleons, now
utterly black, conformed to this. I gave them liquid re-
freshment and a living cricket to each, leaving me with
but six. Down below in the horrid streets, stick figures
were trudging forward stubbornly, resolved to keep their
assignations with old age, sickness, death, and divorce.
Posted at the window, I took my coffee with cream and
aforethought, feeling guilty that I, too, wasn't willing to
endanger myself in city streets. After all, were not these
the same people who afforded me the food and electricity
I couldn't manage without? And the money I had ab-
stracted from the stock market? And might not at least
one of these persons write a decent book someday?

Doubt it but got into my suit anyway and took the
stairway down to about two inches above sea level. It had
not rained during the foregoing black night nor had salt
water intruded into my low-lying neighborhood. Don't be
surprised by the number of people moving back and forth
or that the shops were already open and doing business
enough, one must suppose, to cover their fees, penalties,
assessments, protection, and federal, state, and local taxes.
I waved to a woman standing behind a counter. Someday
a customer might come along. A fat man in an apron was
sweeping in front of a long, dark, and narrow establish-

ment deeded a certain square footage of the clustered city. What were they selling in this place? I yearned to be back in bed again.

I was lucky enough to happen upon an antique shop full of all sorts of things. Could aught be as melancholy and entrancing as a tray of old wedding rings without fingers in them? Fingers enough to reach to the moon and back? Came then an image to mind of my second wife trembling with excitement in her wedding apparel. I entered the place, disturbing the proprietor who wasn't ready for business quiet yet.

"G'morning, my man," said I in my condescending way. For all that I knew, he might have the entire corpus of western literature in his head, his beard was that long. "What do you have for me today?"

He straightened, turned, and looked at me in despair. He was old certainly, and his pupils were out of round. His hand was full of veins, and his eyelids had dust on them. Moving back from me, he spoke something in one or two of his languages. I agreed, offered him a cigarette, and without superintendence proceeded to review the merchandise. It was now past six in the morning and back at headquarters my houseguests would be rising and stretching and running to the toilet.

It startled me to see the things this man had been willing to take on pawn. A saxophone—no surprise there—coats and jackets, a bird cage with a chipmunk in it, polka-dot clown shoes eighteen inches long, a jet engine carburetor, a woodcut illustration of a woman in the buccal position, and many discontinued medicines with peculiar labels on them. One of these, containing a granular solution already half-used-up, did promise to address some of my long-time complaints.

I worked my way among the tarot cards, hideous knives, fifty-year-old comic books, and unmatched socks. There was a World War Two water canteen with blood on it. Ought I not buy the thing and deliver it to the fellow's people? No, it happened long ago, and besides they're mostly dead by now. My notice was taken by a prohibited toy in the form of a grinning negro child munching on a slice of watermelon. There was an oil painting of one of the former presidents attended by a woman wearing kneepads. The sun, frustrated by so many tall buildings, had now begun to nudge up over the horizon. I tried on a baseball cap and then put it back. I was without doubt very close to abandoning the place when I perceived an odd-looking lampshade, somewhat smaller than the average of them, lying at hazard among an unorganized hoard of blankets and bedlinens. Endowed with an unusually keen sense of value, I gathered and appraised it in the weak light prevailing in that part of the shop.

"Odd!" I must have said. Formed from a leathery material of some sort, the shade had shriveled over time, causing the spokes to fall out of skew. There was a tag of about the size of a thumbnail vouching that the object had come from the estate of one *Ilsa Koch*, a German woman I had to presume. Imagine my surprise when I researched that name a week or two later. I expect to get a hundred thousand dollars for it before I die.

I carried my lampshade and medicine to the register and handed over an assortment of small bills published by Taw. The amount was conspicuously greater than required, but the man made no demurral in taking it over into his own possession.

It was tending toward six forty-five when I went back out into the shambolic streets of history's most important city. Eager to get to work on time, the office thralls were leaping from the buses and had formed up in line, each man and woman holding pallid portraits of themselves in front of their faces. Such is the effect of too little sleep on the city's inmates.

Another thousand yards and I'd have reached my favorite bookstore; instead, fearing the sun and unwilling to stroll against the oncoming pedestrians, I turned into a down-and-out cafeteria and meandered to the utmost booth that lay over and against the kitchen itself. It had been years since last I'd dined in a really expensive restaurant and in brief, I had rather eat off the sidewalk than endure the waiters and waitresses that habituate such places. The cook was a fat man in an undershirt who must clearly have had a bad time of it over his six or seven decades of disappointing life. We nodded, each to each. Yes, and I had more lief play a hand of poker with *him* than with anyone reading this.

I ordered two cups of coffee, seasoning one with sugar and the other cream. Hadn't realized how truly hungry I was. The waitress came and smiled, or tried to, and offered me a menu in someone's good handwriting. I was tempted to order half a dozen eggs prepared in a dozen ways, but I'm not *that* evil after all. If only the waitress could have foreseen the enormous gratuity I planned for her, her smile would have been more genuine than it was.

I reckoned her at about forty-five years in age, three children, one divorce, and another on the way. All she had ever wanted was a loving marriage within an organic family but had now finally to admit that the country was well past all that. Her current husband, a decent fellow with six various jobs on his resume, had wanted to see a bit of the world before being harnessed to a complaining wife. The oldest son had gone off to war, returning as an addict with a depressive disease. The daughter was a she-male with a numerous following and very militant. We have no information concerning the youngest of the family. (Facilitator at a transgendering clinic, she told me finally.)

I ordered eggs and grits, the latter of which they had not any. And so I asked for a buttermilk pancake with a fried egg on top. No buttermilk. I asked for the music, odious beyond belief, to be turned down. I asked for a toasted biscuit with true butter and fig preserves; what I got was a fried egg, the broken blister forming a pool of vitelline on the unclean plate. Soon, very soon I would need to take my lustrum holiday back down south again.

Busy with coffee, I hadn't seen that an interracial couple was sitting not fifteen feet from me in a booth of their own. Interracial? I don't mind Mestizos and Jigaboos sitting next to each other, nor Turks and Chinese, but what I saw in front of me that morning was a veritable negro hovering over a pretty little white woman with heart-shaped lips. I'm almost inured by now to those migraines that arrive on wings each time a view of this kind abuts my eyebeams, but this was worse; the negro wore a golden necklace and two earrings inset with purple jaspers. I remembered my old hometown sheriff who had understood how to deal with conduct like that. But how would it be with *you* to catch a white person canoodling with a housefly? That's the effect on me of interracial affairs.

And why were these people up and about at 7:02 in the morning? Habit? Or mental illness? I can almost visualize that primordial malefactor who trained his children to move about in daylight and then go unconscious when the world is lovely and a person's mind is at its best. Here at this hour, there were scapegraces on all sides, adjusters, book keepers, parking meter maids, voters, and sports fans. I detected a fellow citizen who resembled a mole and next to him, a fashion model, or robot, or high school girl. All those jewels and vestments, those shoes and nose rings employed to adorn biological substances yearning for something or another. But now, I must change the direction of my thinking for danger of being thought an unkind person.

I went to the counter to pay for my egg but then jumped back when I saw the woman was Chinese. These people have no emotion you understand and she might just as easily be having an orgasm or appendicitis. We looked at each other across the genomic gulf. I did a little dance to make her smile. The tab was outrageous, of course. Down south, I could have bought the whole chicken for half as much. I took back the tip I had too hastily supplied.

It was daylight in the outside world, and the sun had put on new force. Save for shoppers and the unemployed, the New Yorkers had returned to their cubicles to carry out the functions the economy wants. No doubt these were better than the old-time occupations of grubbing in the soil, contesting with mules, and activities of that sort, but also very inferior to reading and stamp collecting and strolling in the woods. And so why had these people chosen the lesser way? Why do they shy away from music and revolution, man's only true vocations? And why are they interested in each other when not one in ten thousand is more interesting than a discarded cigar? I have myself seen men and women at cocktail parties speaking excitedly of prices, television shows, and peoples' divorces. Herodotus would bore them. Thinking of them and of this epoch, I had one of those revelations that sometimes come to people of my kind, namely that the world was already very ancient and that only those as rare as me could view it *from above*, as it were, and *in retrospect*, so to speak, even *archeologically*, to continue in that vein. I was swept with pity for all living things, innocents bending against the currents of time and age. Said to be too arrogant already, my conceit put on new growth. That was when the snow began to fall.

Eleven

I picked up speed and cut through a clutter of northerners in ludicrous hats. Sans treason, never could the South have lost a war against such people. I followed a dilapidated fat woman for two blocks before diverging in-

to a gigantic department store spilling over with manufactured goods of all sort. Why was I here, here among
crowds of fretful people always racing against the clock?
Afraid to miss the bus or pass up a sale, the richest and
most desperate people on earth.

I roamed the aisles, sometimes following women and
other times tampering with the merchandise. I like to
blow smoke at middle-class women while offering a face
of idiotic innocence. Nothing more dangerous than a man
who is bored, fearless, and brilliant at the same time. I
reckon I must be the dangerest man of them all. I held up
a brassiere for size. One woman laughed, and the other
frowned. I smoked, called out loud for my (second) wife,
and went outside.

The snow had relented somewhat, leaving behind an
inch-thick covering that only partially muffled the never-
pausing traffic. I don't understand snow nor why the Yankee people crave it so. Me, I've always voted for warm
weather, dark nights, and girls with shiny bright eyes.
That moment, I witnessed two pricy automobiles colliding
ineluctably not thirty feet from where I stood. Taking ad-
vantage of the chaos that followed, I entered the scene but
found it impossible to judge the quality of the driver
fighting with his seat belt. Pushed rudely out of range by a
lugubrious policeman with a notable belly, I turned away
in my dignified manner and continued on my way.

I knew that I was coming nigh to a certain hundred-
year-old hotel, my reason for first starting out. Provided
the place were still in business, I planned to climb the
stairs, pull open the massy door embossed in brass, and
then hie me to the bar for a propitious drink with
warmth-giving properties. I had forgot my wallet, of
course, but the bartender could see by looking at me that
my pledge was as good as money. The drink was smooth,
reasonably smooth, or anyway better than nothing. I
viewed a late-middle-age woman stationed at the far end

of the bar, an over-the-hill sort of person with an out-of-focus face who couldn't possibly be anyone other than the daughter of that other unfocused person of thirty-five years ago. No, I was wrong; this one was, or at least had been a male at one time. Her bosom was askew and her nose a bit too bony. As mentioned, the hotel was old, ancient even, and to my great gratitude had made no effort to modernize. I spied a golden spittoon in the corner, used now for an umbrella stand. My heart leap up in joy at the painting over the bar, a palpable nude feasting out of a bowl of juicy grapes. I couldn't vouch for his spiritual quotient, however.

I gave the man my chit but declined the red-headed robot kept behind the bar. Next, I weaved my way to the receptionist and signed the register with my three-hundred-year-old name. I prefer people like myself—silent, gaunt, brilliant, pessimistic, traveled, and unfriendly. Speaking but to him, I mentioned that room of thirty-five years ago while neglecting not to describe the exceptional bathtub and heavy blue drapery that must have weighed two hundred pounds and conceivably did so still.

"With the seascape on it?"

"Yes!"

"All those little ships with . . ."

"Yes!"

". . . red sails?"

"Oh, my goodness yes. I'm so pleased."

"And that great huge old bathtub for honeymoon couples? We had to take that out."

"Now just hold it right there. What did you say? Goddamn it! It never fails, never! Every time something really good comes along, that's when it they take it away!"

"Yes, but life has always been like that. How old are you after all?"

"Goddamn it! Well, what did they do with it?"

"Smelted it down into lots of little bathtubs." He

grinned. "You need to understand, that sucker weighed more than eleven hundred pounds with all that water and people."

I allowed him to assuage my rising anger. He was old, old as me, and had witnessed whole generations passing through his hotel.

"Remember when doctors made house calls?" I inquired.

His eyes brightened.

"And houses had front porches?"

"Those old-time radio shows!"

"They used to deliver milk to our front porches."

"And dogs ran free. I saw it happen."

"And the girls?"

"Don't get me started."

We shed tears. The room I wanted was vacant and the tariff startlingly low for the cost. After our discussion, he was pleased to accept my chit and readily passed over the key, a wooden manufacture—I remembered it well—about ten inches long. And this, too, I remembered: a staircase with a tattered carpet and one missing step. No one doubts that I love old things more than new, but most especially how I adore those greyscale shadows that linger in obsolete hotels. My heartbeat in high gear, I ventured partway down the second level, trying to construct in imagination what sort of persons might be inhabiting the fourteen rooms. Were they as world-weary as they deserved to be? Room number six had a message pinned to the door. Further down, I descried a tricycle lying on its side.

The third and fourth floors were not without features of their own, but I was keen to arrive at my own unforgotten place out of sight of human eyes. There came to me the scent of camphor, mildew, linseed oil, and old lace. At the fifth level, I arrived at a stain glass window picturing Washington and his wife sipping tea, as I supposed, in their vine-covered gazebo. Outside, it was a bright day in New

York City while in Washington's garden the peerless sun burnished the hanging flowers of his second-hand wife.

But now it was time to wait for dark. From habit, I calculated that I had forty-five minutes before the town's big buildings would finally harbor me off from the sun. Already the beams were dissipating, and one could see the photons, if that's what they were, coagulating up and down the hall. Returning to the window, I could see the tops of people's heads, bald people's especially, and could witness their arms swinging back and forth as they locomoted down the walk. Two cars were consulting face to face in the intersection before then braking off and going each in its own chosen direction. This way of life, is it normal? I recollected Hesiod's talk about the pleasures of a good crop and a full barn. And though I could see for miles, not one mule or barn or freckle-face milkmaid came ever into view.

To address this, I left the room and locked it twice. The bellhops were dressed in black, but none were working my floor at this hour. I spied a seam of granulated light in the space between the carpet and the bottom of my neighbor's door. Given my luck, these people might well be Jews. In addition, I have become appreciably incontinent in my old age, and my occasional strolls to Manhattan and back are more perilous than before. I resented having to climb to the eleventh floor to use a toilet. On the other hand, the facility was clean, and only one sole message had been left on the mirror. I peed with constraint as I copied the text on the "back of an envelope," to speak in that way about my deteriorated memory.

I sought the proprietary restaurant and found it at last just next to a man standing in the doorway of a possibly vacant room. Already I had caught scent of the savory, somewhat savory smell that came from the kitchen. Within moments, I would be seated at one of the tables, preferably the one in the corner where my back wouldn't be

available to passersby and whence I could monitor the
people violating my favorite hotel. I saw but one single
waiter, a tall youth in a red jacket who seemed to have
nothing to do. Not a bad job I thought, for those as like to
lucubrate on their feet. I bet he knew the menu upside-
down and had come to abominate people who need half
an hour to choose the nutrients to be turned into manure.

I didn't wait to be seated; I just stood there. A party of
one had taken a table in the exact center of the room and
was munching with extreme slowness on a substance of
some sort. But I wouldn't say he was a depressed sort of
person; on the contrary, he was grinning while he chewed.
A habitual customer I presumed. The sun had greatly declined meantime and was about to fall behind what
looked to me more like a geologic formation than any
garden-variety office complex. Not only had the sun deteriorated, it had given up and was no larger in appearance
than a tiny red seed lodged in space.

A man and woman now entered the room and moved
quietly to a particular place that suggested they had a
claim on it. Such a serene-looking pair of people, I divined
they'd been colluding for ages and needed only the faint-
est of sounds to communicate with each other. Though I
couldn't hear them, I have no quarrel with people of this
type. Satisfied with an average net income, they enjoyed
gardening, Christmas with their children, and had long
ago given up voting. The country could rot for what they
in their wisdom cared. (I did realize, of course, that I was
imputing my own attitudes onto them.) We three, we
knew what life is and what people are, too. I moved quickly to take the adjoining table where I might pick up their
conversational "table scraps," so to speak. Or "so to hear,"
I should have said.

They ordered drinks. The Aryan waiter noted it down
and then scurried off to do what was needed. He also
knew what life is and as one with a less-than-net-average

income, knew about people, too. It came to me that I should have a drink as well, and when my turn came around, I asked for a sloe gin fizz just like the sloe gin fizz my second wife had thought she wanted all those years ago. He didn't tarry, the Aryan, didn't say that he was to be my waiter or that his goal in life was to make me happy. Thus far, the evening had been perfect. By now, the sun had disappeared, but I could still view the profiles of the passers-by, huddled masses yearning to be free. I saw a man in a crumpled hat, fat people, a slue-foot jigaboo fond of sloe gin fizzes, and then a derelict of some description with his face pressed against the glass. Others might have been stock analysts and portfolio managers, word processors, receptionists chosen for their British accents, thousands of lawyers, and a slew of all kinds of other wage earners destined by history to serve the most denatured system the world has seen. Where now are the steamboat captains, tin smiths, and mule skinners of our country's Golden Age?

Just then I caught the words—"It will be alright."—from the next table. Coming closer, I learned there had been a problem with the couple's first-born, a seventeen-year-old dropout with a lot of tattoos. However, they had talked it over with his counsellors, and now it was going to be alright. I nodded and smiled and toasted the woman in confirmation of her opinion. But they were in the twenty-first century now, and it was highly unlikely that her children or anyone else's could ever be alright again.

I was served with a savory meal of miscellaneous seafoods, the scallops deserving special praise. Less attractive were the shrimps in fetal position, some with their intestinal tracts still intact. A few other diners, two of them Jews, had entered in the meantime and after some discussion, had chosen the tables most commensurate with them. The rain had by no means slackened; on the contrary, it had strengthened, and in more than one case I could see people sprinting through the downpour as if they still hoped to keep themselves dry. I love to watch women moving back and forth in their funny bodies. An elderly investor just then slipped and fell. I had to laugh at that. A man of my type welcomes all things nature inflicts upon other people. I then saluted (he couldn't see me) a Caucasian youth moving forward complacently with a guitar. Alabama has many of these.

That moment, a jagged bolt of lightning plunged into the East River and never came out again. This was followed by the expected thunder that to me always announces the moment a little white girl is being molested by a jigaboo. My mind leaped back to 1928 when my old grandfather had participated in a flaying bee still sometimes mentioned in the neighborhood. The rain now began truly to come down, but I didn't plan on getting wet. I had expected the sloe fizz to be unpleasant, but by means of my exceptional will, I was able to choke it down at last. The diners, perhaps a dozen of us by now, were watching each other closely.

The cashier was a standard person, but I had to dicker with her over the fare. I needed to micturate, too, but the place was on the eleventh floor. Slowly, I began the climb. No one could be brave enough to use *that* elevator. I stepped past an elderly resident experiencing trouble with his crutches. I helped him to the next landing where he could rest for as long as he desired. A magazine was there for his convenience as also an ashtray in the form of a frog with a gaping mouth. This fellow hadn't been in the outside world for ages past; my own sort of hotel absolutely.

I waited in line and at length was allowed to urinate, also at length. The room now had a fresh graffito in it, obscene beyond description. There was a bathtub, too, unusably small compared to the giant one of thirty-five years ago. Life is strange. I used to be on the forefront of time, a darling youth always in trouble with normal things and people.

The bed that I had been given? The best thing in the whole building. Charlemagne would have knighted the yeoman who offered it him. The television, thankfully, was turned to the wall. I knew the function these things serve at the behest of government in rented rooms. Better was the view from my window, a pink and green smear of blinking neon lamps promoting services and products best ignored. I smoked. As you have seen, I had brought no books, and all too quickly I had read all the warning labels and every bit of tourist information the place afforded.

An hour at the window and it was time for bed. I was grateful for the quilts that promised to be sufficient even in this unheated building. The night was dark and black, and very little light came from the nearby buildings that also were mostly black and dark. Had Manhattan lost its electricity? No, the pink and green neon haze continued pulsing from the business district. I crept between the sheets, embroidered products left over from the previous century. But I would have to wait for day to see the sort of patterns that embellished them. Someone, a girl I believed, let out a brief scream from one of the lower floors. I received a phone call that I ignored. I was sure that I had turned that machine to the "off" position, still a permissible action even in the northern states. Came now the time to sleep.

I dreamt I was looking into the face of a grinning dog, and then next that the rain had resumed in New York City, a prevision that proved to be true when I got out of bed and went to check on it. I then slept more or less solidly for two to three hours before having to abandon bed and hurry up to the eleventh floor for the toilet. A child was splashing about in that bathtub that certainly *I* wouldn't have chosen to use. He grabbed for his yellow rubber duck to prevent me taking it. A derelict was sleeping in the hall, his scarecrow's body blanketed in sheets of the world's most appalling newspaper.

Someone had been in my room but had left my shoes and cellphone behind. I filled the pitcher and drank from it. A single black fly was trudging an inch per hour across the plaster ceiling. I had no books. Finally, I took out my sniffing glue and arranged it on the floor within reach of my most proximate arm.

I dreamt that I was in attendance at my old high school reunion and everyone was laughing at me. I used to be in love with Sheila, never knowing she was a Jew. Apart from the waiters, there were no black people in those days, and I was willing to check my Glock at the door. There was no possible reason for my first wife to have been there—she was always out of kilter with that time and place—but we chatted briefly all the same.

Twelve

I woke early, dressed and peed and packed my kit. I made my bed and cleaned the room, unwilling to leave that tedious job to underpaid women. I assembled my semiautomatic and silencer and slipped it into the clothen holster stitched inside my double-breasted suit. I use a soft ammunition, the so-called RIP standard that knows how to chase through bodies shredding organs as it travels. As to the silencer, the thing has sponge-like baffles that reduce 9-millimeter noise to a child-like sneeze. Any other hotel and I would have left without paying, but not so here in my last sanctuary in this loathsome city.

"I want to thank you for your hospitality," said I to the assumed anti-Semite who took my chit.

"Are you going out . . . *there*?" he asked, nodding to the indicated place.

"I must."

"Why not just stay here with the rest of us?"

"Hm. It's worth considering. I'll think about it."

"No, you won't."

We shook. His eyeballs were grey instead of white, the fruit of his years on Fifty-Second Street. I left the building and proceeded more or less steadily for about two hundred yards before taking a rest. As to the people, there must have been a hundred thousand of them between my home and me. I found myself walking stride for stride with one of the Pk47 robots carrying a newspaper under his arm. I don't suppose I'll ever accustom myself to these developments. The younger brother of Fred Reeves has actually murdered a robot, and that case is *still* tied up in court.

Was I really prepared to use that unsteady footbridge over the East River? The more I thought about it, the more slowly I plodded forward. My old brain then summoned up Spengler's dictum about the end of things. A sneaker shop hove into view, scores of pathogenic negroes scrambling over the merchandise. For such as these, slavery would offer an undeserved promotion. I passed between tall buildings occupied by prosperous people consecrated to buying and selling things produced by others. I detoured around a policeman twirling a blunt-force baton on an alligator thong. The automobiles, a heterogenous congregation, were barking at each other non-stop. An ambulance dashed by with an arm and two legs hanging out. I saw human happiness lying in the gutter with a stock certificate driven through her heart. Old enough am I to remember women who yearned for hearth and home, husband and dog, and a well-built barn; today, their grandbabies are frantic for positions, promotions, titles, and a third-floor corner office. I used to fear that America might soon collapse; now I fear it won't.

I do admit that some of the buildings were attention-worthy and seemed to be well-constructed, but these were interlarded with a great many others that together formed an incongruous mess. Were it Trevelyan who wrote that prior to the Industrial Revolution, the West had been largely beautiful? I plodded on. In front, the cold-weather sun had begun rotating almost imperceptibly, a slow-motion roulette forecasting wealth for whom God adores.

I was still a good many blocks from the footbridge and by no means certain I could reach it before my leg fell out from under me. Held together with a cadmium plate no thicker than a dime, I had spent fifty-three years waiting for the bone to give out. I smoked two cigarettes consecutively without catching the attention of the police. And, too, I was carrying twenty-four rounds of ammunition distributed between several pockets.

For these and two or three other reasons, I turned in at the first coffee shop and sped towards the men's facility. A three-hundred-pound black individual was roosting on the toilet. Lest I wished to explode, I had no option but to seek surcease at the sink, a lengthy operation that seemed to exasperate those still waiting in line. The graffiti was everywhere, some of it formed out of spray paint almost impossible to remove. A big-city pervert was hunkered in the corner, grinning.

It had been my intention to invest in a cup of coffee, a slice of pie mayhap, a cinnamon roll perhaps, but the clientele caused me to reconsider. There were at least two surly little Jews complaining at the counter, their pudgy fingers decorated with ruby rings. Really, didn't they now regret having left their homeland in the Mesopotamian East? Certainly, I did. And to think that golden Alexander could have so easily absolved us of this!

Smiling into the CCTV cameras, I went one further block and then stopped to call my colleague Gretel who was in Europe as it proved. By contrast, Frank was home—he always was—and when I described my situation, my leg and headache and the rest, he asked for just fifteen minutes to arrive at my location at the corner of two named streets. I had brought no books, and so to waste the time, I simply stood without moving beneath the awning of a dress shop where numbers of postmodern women were agonizing in front of the shoe displays. No wonder my marriages never succeeded. What goes on in those adorable people? Really, oughtn't they have window panes in the back of their heart-shaped heads?

I watched and smoked and sometimes came out to check on the sun. Perhaps the thing had blinked out several minutes ago, but the dark hadn't come down to us just yet. And someday would come great balls of fire to burn the city away. Frank arrived late, and at first, I pretended not to notice him. Fifteen minutes, he had promised. I hadn't seen him in weeks, and he looked chronologically older now. He had brought a bottle for my headache, and I swigged at it gratefully. Unfortunately, he had something of Mozart's on the machine but then quickly shut it off when he saw my face.

"And so, you still feel obliged to come to Manhattan and walk around from time to time."

I admitted it. "I want to be able to describe it to my descendants."

"You don't have any descendants!"

"I have one."

"Oh, for God's sakes; you're not going to bring *that* up again!"

"He *might* be mine."

"And he might be dead. I used to think that you and [second wife] might have children."

I said nothing. Any child of hers and mine might really have been that new Alexander come to save the West. With her looks and birth canal and my qualities already described, no one can ever know.

"She wants to get back in touch with you, is what I hear."

I said nothing once again. We were moving through a

transactional urban waste famous for its felonies. And yet, real estate prices in this vicinity had expanded beyond the power of mathematics. My poor grandfather had enjoyed better scenery during his sharecropper days.

"What's the scenery from *your* apartment," I asked.

"We use television for that."

The man had four books on the passenger side floor, giving me no reason to insult his literary tastes. I jumped back, astonished to see that he had actually somehow acquired a faultless copy of the first run of Moulston's *Sins and More*.

"How on earth . . . ?"

"Leave it alone. It's mine."

That moment, I perceived a small voice from the back seat. I jumped back, having not suspected, or not until now anyway, that the man's wife was with us.

"He's so jealous of it," she said.

I turned and gazed at her for longer than I should. She was a decent-looking quantity even if somewhat too bosom-deprived for my liking. And of course, she had that New York twang.

"Very decent-looking," said I to Frank. "Does she share our feelings about the Ashkenazim?"

They broke out laughing, husband and wife.

"Does she? You're an amateur compared to her."

I offered her a cigarette and asked her to come sit in my lap.

They dwelled, and still do, in an upper-story four-room containment adorned with the famed 1932 Dietrich Eckhart daguerreotype. Together, we examined it for a period. The furniture was tatty, but the drapes quite thick enough to shut off the landscape. If there were any closed-circuit cameras in the apartment, they were well-disguised.

I was allowed to review their book hoard, perhaps 500 epicene volumes in maintained bindings. This is where their money went. And so, they read Russian, too, the rascals. My opinion of the pair was escalating rapidly. In truth, the lady did have an almond-shaped face with Slavic eyes. More than that, she also possessed two of more appealing buttocks recently seen by me. A third would have been too much.

"Who despises Kikes the most?" I speculated. "Russians or Germans?"

"Ukrainians."

"A noble folk!"

I accepted the drink that was offered. I'm not allowed to consume more than a certain amount of daily alcohol, but I had been saving up for a long while. The olive had sunk to the bottom, but I was able to spear it with my ballpoint pen.

"Okay, apart from Germans and Russians and Ukrainians, who detests the Jews most of all?"

"The Jews!"

It was a good one and almost certainly true. We laughed, we three, till the sky began to darken, and I had perforce to repair to the toilet. Finished with that, I secured the five rooms on this floor and rejoined my hosts. I have not described Frank, which in any case wouldn't be needed if you had seen him. His wife is and was as above described. But now the evening was drawing on, and we three had spent more than an hour cerebrating quietly in the dark. After two drinks, the atmospherics in the room had turned sodden and in the case of Frank, truculent even.

"Slow-motion genocide," he said. "But what race of men ever did better? And will they finally be happy when we're gone?"

"The only way they can be happy," I inserted, "is for us to be Jews and them to be normal. But I'm not waiting for that."

"Those old Australopiths, *they* were happy. They didn't want to become extinct either."

In this way passed the time. Shortly after ten, an elderly anti-Semite stopped by to share a bag of fresh-baked
powdered doughnuts. The items were warm and soft, and
I took two. Coming near, he bent and squinted at me for
the space of a few seconds. The light was poor, and his
eyes were, too. But he retained more than half of those
doughnuts when he left us.

I was given one of the very rooms I had inspected earlier. Though I prefer rectangular spaces proportioned
roughly like a poker card, I couldn't complain. The cell
was clean, certainly, and the window too narrow to admit
a full-grown person. After twenty-four hours "on the
road," so to speak, I was avid for some good reading. Just
half an hour later and after having dropped off to sleep, I
arose, forced open the door, and then traipsed ever so quietly to the library where to my amazed surprise the couple
was sleeping on the carpet beneath a simple sheet that
didn't altogether cover them. More than a year was to pass
before I learned that they possessed but the one bed only.

There was light enough to let me choose my reading
matter for the remainder of the night—volume three in
Hodgkin's *History of Italy and Her Invaders*, a neglected
classic I encourage you to read. The floor was hard, and I
could not rightly understand how my hosts even with all
their courtesy to guests were prepared to lie upon it all
night long. My bed could easily have accommodated all of
us. As to the book, I found that it held a letter in green
ink, a superannuated relic, browned and brittle, between
pages 335 and 336. I did not choose to read it, of course, as
I could not in good conscience do so.

The writer's mother had died one day earlier and the
recipient, whoever it might have been, was being notified
forthwith of the funeral two days hence. They didn't tarry,
those old people, when it came to shoveling people into
the ground. The letter affected me; I admit it. A thousand
years might go by, but never would I set eyes on the au-

thor of that letter nor her mother neither. I would wager my body parts that they had been better people than those snoring down in the library at this time.

I had anticipated that I wouldn't be able to read legibly at this late hour and had been right to think so. The print was old and every two or three sentences boasted an obsolete word. Nor was the typeface terribly appealing. Instead, I smoked. It is true that my modern telephone had my second wife's number in it, but I opted not to call her at this time. No doubt she was lodged in one of those tall apartment buildings just across the river where very likely she had fallen to sleep with her bedside lamp still burning. She would have aged, of course, but I didn't expect her to be significantly less attractive than at the beginning. To enter those buildings and search her down would need more time than I had.

As we should have expected, I got very little sleep that night. Lacking an ashtray, I tried to flush a number of cigarette stubs at the same time, creating a mess on the floor. My patience at an end, I then roused my hosts and politely explained how normally I took coffee at this hour. The man, confused seemingly, got slowly into his shoes followed by his socks. Outside, the snow-white sun was but a tiny punctuation mark at the start of day. An ambulance went by at high speed, the first of a predictable five or six. I envisioned the patient, an elderly lady dead five minutes ago. Ten minutes and millions of little creatures begin feasting.

I never smile.

I walked home under my own power, my hosts allowing me to depart without a fight. I noted a man with an accordion stationed on the corner, a beggar supposedly. We looked at each other. The CCTV cameras were particularly abundant in this region, but I was able without undue effort to avoid being entailed by them. A more difficult matter, the iris recognition registers were everywhere.

Just then a well-dressed northeastern sort of person stepped in front of me and tried to initiate a conversation concerning a new iteration of his company's standard health and home repair software. A child was sitting on the curb, but I managed to get past her and her mangy dog without contributing a single sou to the pathetic little cup resting in her lap. I caught elements of a discussion emanating from someone's escrubilator. No, it was my own device urging me to take my serotonin prescription. Striving to obey the command, I collided into a tiny person who called my name. Everybody knows everything these days. Myself, I put on a neutral expression, my habitual maneuver whenever I'm north of Tennessee.

You wouldn't think a person could be pleased when a building as drear as mine comes into view. Maintaining my facial expression, I threw myself up the stairs, urinated, fed the lizards, and then prepared an alcoholic beverage that my doctor would have abominated. One of the anti-Semites was in the parlor, asleep amid a heap of cultural equipment. I examined my freezer, finding a gallon of ice cream not bought by me. The pantry was also full. It was my very own home containing my own very bed and accustomed toilet. Ended thus my next-to-last excursion to Manhattan and back.

I drank a little too much and then visited the pink room and parleyed briefly with a European guest, an educated Swiss having problems adapting to America. A new organization offering sanctuary to anti-Semites had been established in the German part of his country, and my friend had come hither for funding. I rendered him a good-size check needless to say, and then sent him off to bed. Someone had been in my room but had restored each and every object to its right location. Suddenly, I jerked away the quilt lest someone had deposited a snake between the sheets, my involuntary habit since college days.

I chose my reading matter. From two flights below,

there came the nightly noise of bad behavior from the "bawdy house" staffed by licensed robots. Ironic when compared and contrasted to the always-silent Carthusian Monastery on the fifteenth floor. All in all, the building comprised forty-two floors, people living on top of each other. The Greeks would have been appalled.

A plane flew over, adding to the everlasting noise from the robots. Instead of a snake, I lifted a deceased mouse from the sheets and carried it to the paper shredder. I took my pills, organizing them by color and size prior to tossing them two at a time down my gullet. A tiny dose of succinylcholine should guarantee a good night's sleep, as I mistakenly believed.

Now I could read. And actually, did do so for about a page and a half till the drug and my exhaustion escorted me to a mental state where right away I began rummaging through some of my favorite dreams. In my cloudy condition, I thought I saw a stick of crumpled lightning plunge into a building across the street. Three-fourths asleep, I had sense enough to extinguish my cigarette thank goodness, extinguishing it by error on the quilt as I realized later. A bee had become trapped in the doorknob and was making a furious noise.

I dreamt that it was raining, the most enjoyable of all sounds apart from Wagner and Mahler and one or two others. And was it also raining in Trinidad where prudent people were locked away in their cozy chambers? I felt a kinship with all non-Jewish people everywhere, deep-sea divers and lighthouse keepers especially. I felt for the birds and monkeys sheltering beneath the leaves. I even felt for the little fleas and termites who had no sleeping place one-tenth as good as mine.

It's no great distance from imagining that it's raining to raining really. I leapt to the window, cheered to see that already a few little puddles had formed on the sidewalk and in the road. I do understand that the polar ice caps are not predicted to melt *entirely* during our lifetimes, hers and mine, but who can anticipate the *rainfall*? I have read of the everlasting precipitation of liquid methane on other planets and envisioned the elite of New York City ecstasizing over hydrocarbon cocktails at their parties.

In sympathy with the rain, I had unwittingly drenched my underwear, all the excuse I needed to shower. But first, I called for my chameleons and teased them with my fingertip. My favorite, Edmund, possesses non-coordinated eyes that can scan 270 degrees from a stationary position. I try to imagine the images impinging all at once on that tiny brain. His mouth is wide, his tongue is long, and his horn is blunt. Give him the dimensions of a man and he'd govern the earth.

I cut a piece of pie and went to the window to nibble on it. The rain was continuing, albeit too indifferently to do serious harm to the acreage down below. Is it possible we anti-Semites might cause this place to drop more quickly beneath the waves by jumping up and down on it? Don't be absurd. Better to wait for those great waves of fire to come rolling in from the Poconos.

It *will* happen. More immediately, I had 219 unanswered calls on my telephone, all but one of them a solicitation. There was a summons from Rodney Quartz (his real name oddly enough) for a get-together at The Asphalt Maze (his favorite tavern) this very afternoon. Lloyd had produced a new version of our journal and needed a decision as to the design and date of release. I had already learned from Fred that the magazine might include numbers of anti-Semitic cartoons done by one of our colleagues in Nevada, a draftsman of real talent. I do not believe a better pornographic artist exists anywhere. Next, I called my broker to learn that I had become $17,000 richer during my sojourn in Manhattan. Had I actually accomplished anything during that time, I would likely be poorer.

At 10:07, I replaced the batteries in my security camera,

put a grain of rice on my doorknob, and was about to use the elevator when I caught sight of a third-generation robot hunkered in the corner. The stairs were free, however, and I was actually able to reach the lobby before the machine. It's not often that these things abandon their work places, and when they do, they usually wear sunglasses to obscure their non-verisimilitudinous eyes. And then, too, they have an especial fear of rain shorting their circuits. I stay far away from them, of course, conscious as I am of the penalties for abridging their civil rights.

Today, the city appeared so much older, as if in a nineteenth-century photograph, or as when one is driving through the rain. The pedestrians were few and far apart, and their umbrellas looked like a highway of lily pads. If Time shall have an aftermath, it will look like this.

I had intended to badger my Jewish broker, an obsequious man startlingly reminiscent of Wagner's Mime; instead, I swerved off at Zack Taylor Avenue and drove to that notoriously-dilapidated theatre where old black and white films were constantly on offer. My memory is so poor by now, I can view these productions for the tenth time and still find them as fresh as when they were issued. The audiences are generally thin, of course, but the films are good.

I parked at the rear of the building and used an entrance known only to a few. Amazingly, a viewer can smoke cigarettes in this place and acquire alcoholic beverages along with the popcorn. He could position himself, the viewer, where no one else was within a certain perimeter. That person could even fall off to sleep and stay in that condition for long periods. Apart from my favorite hotel, it was the noblest place in all the northeastern states. I won't try to recite the name of this film which anyway I don't remember, though I do very clearly recall the face of the actress with her rosy lips and golden hair. In which cemetery is she lying now, her lips all eaten away and her hair turned to fungi? A man might detest 98% of life on earth while still harboring a soft spot for women who were lovely once.

I stayed until almost noon, lunching on a frankfurter with sauerkraut and a cup of wine. I'm not saying the actress was a good person; I simply do not know. In addition to this, the theater had numerous restrooms offering people of my sort a sense of security. Traipsing back to the counter for a vanilla pudding, I verified that the rain was continuing and that the passers-by were notably fewer now. I observed a taxi running through the puddles and a bright yellow umbrella bumping down the sidewalk. As for me, I might stay in this warm place for as long as I wist. I never get bored, not so long as I can sit quietly in the dark critiquing my heartbeats and digestive music. True, I had brought neither pillow nor book, but I did have a device in my head that contained dozens of classic texts.

I awoke at 1:50 and made an attempt to rise. The rain had lessened, but I remained unwilling to leave the building. I was able to speak by phone with our cartoonist in Nevada who reported that the temperature in his area was an envious 64°. In any case, another film was showing just then, a historical drama featuring some really fine-looking Elizabethan women in costumes and jewels.

I departed the place before sundown and drove westward between the overlapping shops and apartment buildings. I try to remember the moments of my declining life in case later on someone wants my personal information. "The moon was at about a 30° angle with the Chrysler Building," I might say. Or, "that ape that escaped last Tuesday from the zoo is waiting at the corner for the light to change." Just then a telephone call came through which I ignored. I was playing the Klemperer rendition of Mahler's *Abschied* and admit to being distracted by the music, the traffic, my bladder, neon, and the stars. I shall never understand why we great ones have to travel instead of just relocating ourselves to destinations by force of mind alone.

My own destination proved to be a rich-looking district designed for talk show hosts, pornographic stars, investment bankers, and the like. I parked at a distance and approached warily. There was an iron knocker at the door, a brawny fixture as heavy as an anvil. A medium-size anvil. I employed it just once creating a somewhat disappointing sound akin to the clash of an iron spoon on dinnerware of like material.

I entered a beautifully-furnished drawing room that was perhaps a bit too narrow and then stood quietly examining the dozen or so framed paintings along the walls. A few minutes having passed, I then went back outside and waited to be admitted. Least of all had I expected *Gretel* to come to the door. She's a good deal shorter than me, and her nose comes up only to the top button of my dress shirt which it resembles somewhat.

"Gret!" said I. She was in an outfit that sorted with her gender. "I would have brought a gift, if I'd known you'd be here."

"Not too late," she said, trying to disguise her northern accent.

"Who are our speakers tonight?"

"Frank gave a really wonderful talk but then had to hurry off to the airport. Aren't you coming in? I want to show you my new painting."

"Wonderful. But this isn't, like, you know, *your* place now is it?"

"Hardly!" She laughed. She had perhaps three fillings among her lower jaw though these didn't interfere overmuch with her general dentition. Her nostrils had been trimmed and the openings were perfect circles. "No, we're just living together these days, Frank and I."

"Good, good." (Frank? That poltroon was unquestionable the very worst of our local anti-Semites.)

"But it could have been you."

"What!" (I swayed and almost fainted.)

"But I couldn't bear to hurt Griselda," she claimed, citing the pseudonym of my second wife.

"Oh, for God's sakes, I wouldn't of ever told her!"

"Wouldn't '*have*' ever told her. Your grammar, tsk, tsk, tsk."

"My grammar is better than Frank's! But are you *never* going to fetch me a drink?"

She went to get it. I could descry a fair number of guests in the adjoining room, some of them well known to me and others much less so. "There's ole Taw!" I uttered happily, pleased to see his oft-mistaken figure in the doorway. The music was good, something of Smetana's as I rightly guessed. These were the best people in the world, informed Aryans capable of the most extreme viciousness when it came time to expand one's tribal promptings.

I smoked. It was early yet, and the usual alcohol, drug, and tobacco proctors were still somewhat loath to enter private quarters. I noticed but refused to pay much attention to what either was a transgendered "skin job," or a *New York Times* columnist approaching from across the room. I had not time enough mentally to place myself elsewhere.

"Hey! I *know* you," the creature said, striving to hide his tic. Tics. He had a beverage in one hand and another in the other.

"You actually going to drink that?" I asked, pointing to each of his beverages in turn. Drunk already, or almost, for a long time he stood staring down at the two nearly identical mixtures. I drifted toward where good conversation might be on offer but ended up instead amid a rabble of anti-Semites rummaging through a crate of art objects that Reece had brought back from New Orleans. I lifted a 6.5 Creedmoor fitted with an elevated telescopic sight and a double silencer almost the size of a baseball bat. The laser produced a tiny red dot on Clarence Sizemore's unlovely moustache, but I quickly pushed the gun away when I saw it was making him nervous.

"Good choice," Reece allowed. "That darling can kill at six hundred yards while making a noise no greater than an acorn."

"*Six hundred*?"

"Believe it. I can blow a cantaloupe apart at *eight* hundred."

"Baal! And you chose a cantaloupe because it's about the size of a human head, right?"

"Slightly smaller than an Ashkenazi head actually. If I can do a cantaloupe at eight hundred, I don't expect any difficulty with actual three-dimensional Jews."

Others now began to gather around. He had no choice, Reece, but to demand market price for his merchandise though he did offer discounts to the young ones among us, even passing over free of charge a Smith & Wesson .357 magnum semi to a new member, a college student finishing a history degree. The boy hefted it once or twice and broke into a smile.

Taw, who actually had murdered a Jew (albeit with a car instead of a gun) bought four of the things along with a gross of hollow-point ammunition. Myself, I generally prefer a more intellectual sort of weaponry, but I was beginning to see the temptation of physically disassembling those who wish to demote the superior race to minority standing in our own private country. In some instances, punishments may be too severe while for others no conceivable penalty can be enough. I give you this—should a white man be punished as rigorously for the murder of a jigaboo as the other way around? Someday, you'll be able to vote on this.

I already possessed a decent number of handguns, two of them with high-grade mufflers, but to kill silently at *half-mile distances* couldn't be resisted. In the end, I bought a 50-caliber Regulator with a five-power scope along with 500 rounds of steel-jacketed combat-grade ammunition. A lovely artifact, I aimed it at various people in the room and then went about to show it to the girls.

"Like to make a cheese souffle out of Ashkenazi brains?" I asked, allowing them to touch the thing. There was no question it had an appeal for some of them; indeed, I thought for a moment that Hilda Jaeger was about to take the barrel into her lovely mouth and suck on it. Not as adorable as my second wife, she had turned out even better with respect to the Jewish Question. Her bosoms were rich and deep and culminated in two blunt nozzles presumably pink. Not that ever *I'd* be allowed to toy with them at any length. We danced briefly; her conversation was mediocre, however. But among women, intellect is just a memetic activity after all.

It wasn't till well after dark that I discovered the bar. I requested a daiquiri and consumed it rapidly and while waiting for the effect to become affect I drifted to the dining room where Alois and two others unknown to me were pouring over a pilot edition of our new journal, *The Heartland Review* as they had named it. Adorned with an uncommon cover, it was a portentous-looking affair holding a dozen articles, a short story, the photo of an underrated dictator, and four extremely well-drafted colored cartoons contributed by one of our members in Nevada. I was impressed. If the censors weren't sufficiently alert, I saw no reason why this publication might not find subscribers and even be given space in churches, airports, and waiting rooms.

"My God," said I to Alois. "This is just superb. An elixir for awakened people! But who will read it?"

He blushed with deserved pride. "We have a list."

"Indeed?"

"But postage, don't you know. The cost just gets worse

and worse."

He looked at me, I looked at him. Recognizing what he was saying, I took out a check and jotted down a goodly amount on it, flabbergasting the man. A non-alcoholic sort of person, he lifted his Root Beer, I believe it to have been, and quaffed at it saying, "Gosh! Thanks a lot!"

"How long before you can send out the first issue?" I inquiringly asked.

He grinned. "May 1st!"

Do any of my readers not know meaning of that date?

Thirteen

You should know that Alois has an in-law who serves as the crime reporter for one of New York's more gruesome newspapers. My friend learned from him just last week that a seventeen-year-old white prostitute with a habit and two fatherless children had been found lodged underneath an old Ford car in a disused parking lot. Her eyes had been removed and her mouth filled with feces. Death had finally come from an icepick in her prefrontal cortex.

"A *white* woman?" we asked.

"White as she could be."

I couldn't forget about it. Three days went by (one of them accompanied by decent rain) whereafter we met again in our special location.

"Have they caught the nigger yet?" we asked.

"Oh, yes. Caught him real quick, too. Bobby Flynn tracked him down in Canarsie and put the cuffs on him. But the judge wants to let him go."

"What!"

"Racism. Bobby bruised his arm."

We gathered around the no-longer-used wood-burning stove that had come to represent a sort of family hearth for us racists. The Finnish man had learned enough lan-

guage by now to appreciate what had been said. His face
turned beet red, and his kneecaps were trembling.

"Well, where the devil *is* he then!" Muldany asked.

"Patience. But first, let's have a round of drinks."

We ordered and drank while the man called James
Quast, a blood-splatter analyst not known to me earlier,
took out his phone and made a call. I could not translate
the respondent's voice. The phone itself was dark blue and
possessed a new-style antenna that yawed automatically
toward the incoming voice. The music, of poor quality,
came from a section of the enormous room that I could
not easily make out in the general gloom. It was dark outside and dark, too, in the inner restaurant where a few
widely-separated mixed-race couples were consuming
their suppers in a spirit of reciprocal hostility. I believe I've
already said that the sight of negroes canoodling with
white girls has an effect on me.

"Well, where the devil *is* he then!" Muldany reiterated
faultlessly.

It developed, we belatedly learned, that Bobby had in-
tended to arrest the man and carry him down to the station to fill out the forms, etc., etc., but then at a late moment had turned aside and conveyed the prisoner to a
wooded location some twenty miles northwest of Yonkers.
I expect the negro was getting nervous by this time.

"Yo, dog," he was said to have said. "What's this shit?
Bunch of ole mother-fucking trees? Sheet mon, we got
rules in this country!"

"Don't stop now," we begged our interlocutor.

"Okay, turns out that son-of-bitch got lashed to a tree
with three handcuffs linked end to end and . . ."

"Wait a minute, hold it; how did he get the cuffs away
from Bobby?"

"Did I say that? Did I say the nigger got the cuffs off
Bobby? I don't think so. No, it were *Bobby* what tied that
bastard to the tree."

"And left him there to starve. Right?"

"Did I say that? I don't think so. That wouldn't have been very nice would it? No, he went back to town to pick up five gallons of kerosene."

"Oh, oh."

"Can't 'pick' that stuff up! That's one of the first things I ever learned."

"Shut up, Charley. We want to hear this."

"Kerosene. He already had the matches don't you see."

(Do readers want me to continue this?)

"Christ!"

"Took him all morning to use it up."

"Oh, shit. And I thought *I* was hard."

"Want to see what happened?"

"I'll pass."

I also preferred to go home. Instead, we paid the bill—the two policemen were not charged—and then loaded ourselves into four of the cars parked about and began the long journey westward to the wildlife preserve called *Beauregard Hallows*. It was an extensive drive, and the radio music was not, believe me, of the best quality. But it was a policeman's vehicle after all. One of them was going through a divorce and had no wish to speak while the other, a much younger sort was perpetually muddling with his latest-version telephone. He seemed to have acquaintances everywhere, including in Britain apparently. This instrument also gave off music and had a tiny geo-device to show where we were going.

The gate was, of course, locked at this hour, but we had those policemen with us. A one-lane gravel road led to a dirt trail scarce broad enough to permit an automobile. We continued on, the path growing more and more narrow and the music worse and worse till finally we left the car and walked in single file to the place of execution. I was not entirely sure I wanted to see this. But what the hell after all? The burnt man would have to serve in lieu of all those other African people who, suffering from evolutionary lacunae feel impelled to harm superior people.

We came from different directions. The burnt man was wearing an expression that resembled an upside-down smile and let me say here and now that it were better never to have seen the sun than to have sampled one-tenth of what this gentleman had endured. He had a tennis ball in his mouth and from the waist down, he had turned to charcoal amongst which glimpses of white bone could be seen. But it was *above* the belt that the work of true evil was on view. The man had once had iron buttons to hold his coat together but these had fully melted leaving silver rills down a bark-like torso not three-fourth its original size. The lymph and other fluids that facilitate the life of a human had formed three little puddles on the cold hard ground. The police were the first to abandon the scene followed soon after by the photographer and finally we racists last of all.

Hoping to bypass the anti-white press, we took a different route back to Manhattan where already the first drunks and businesspersons were marching up and down in search of . . . God wat not.

Fourteen

And so, this then is how the notion gained force—that we could assail our enemies on two fronts at once. First, we weaken them with intellectual argument and then destroy at least some portion of the Judeo-African demographic by force of force. We had the marksmen and we had the long-range rifles. We had a date and we had New York City spread out in front of us like a five-course meal. The thought of it made me smile again, the first time since my divorce. But first, we must bring some of our less valiant members around to the Committee's decision, Tay presiding.

Speaking to the seventy to eighty members meeting in the back room of our chosen restaurant, he described a downtown synagogue frequented by some of the most feculent kikes in the city. He spoke of that elephantine newspaper striving to launch a final solution of the white question. He spoke of other things as well. "Let us kill," Tay said, "just fifty or sixty of these things, and half a million will emigrate."

I ejaculated, the first time since my divorce. To be honest, I wasn't so certain that as many as that would actually go away and leave us alone, no, we'd need to slay at least five hundred to eventuate *that*. I glanced to Lloyd standing nearby with his wife, his face and hers contorted with delight. We drank and chatted and lauded Tay, already our bespoken leader, and then broke into committees to manage the details. My assignment? I was to preview a secondary target (assuming we survived our first action) namely that downtown brokerage with the famous name, a hallowed establishment consecrated to manipulating sovereign debt and currency futures. Yes, I knew the place quite well.

I slept that night in episodic fashion and then left the bed at 3:15 to take two dopamine capsules. Someone was stirring in one of the downstairs rooms. The rain had *not* continued. Going to my narrow window, I chose to imagine that I could see human silhouettes jumping up and down on the roofs of the faraway buildings. Bored and restless, I foddered my salt-water fish and enjoined them to remember me kindly once I be dead.

The gibbous sun arrived off-schedule and bore a liverish look. I dressed and packed my kit, postponing until next day my coffee and scheduled bowel movement. I freshened my bullets but left my identifications behind. Finally, with the sun still jittering back and forth among the clouds, I sallied forth into the confused streets of the waning city where a riot or perhaps a celebration of some sort had broken out over at the Cambodian Containment. I scurried past hastily, keeping my white face out of sight. Having forgotten myself, I took out a cigarette but managed to toss it away before being ticketed.

I had not traveled by subway for the longest time. The platform supported a large number of odd-looking young people with attention-summoning hairdos and glabrous faces. I found a seat on starboard side where the travelers, some of them, scored as much as a "seven" on my personal ten-scale. But even here there were tattoos, obesity, pregnancies, and viruses of every sort. I homed in on a flitch of meat sitting just across from me, a fifty-year-old female wishing I would look elsewhere. It was impossible to decode the graffiti rushing past though I did descry one particularly well-drawn image of an attractive woman engrossed in an oral activity. From the intercom, we learned of the advance of the Polish Zloty on the Forex exchange. We stopped to pick up a testy-looking negro with bright red eyes. He was thinking of murdering us all, never imagining that that distinguished-looking man sitting off by himself had a 9mm Glock in his ankle holster. I urged him, begged him really, to make the attempt.

It is my hope that historians living a thousand years hence will say no more about the West after about 1960. At that date, even Britain might have gone down with a decent reputation. I left the train, weaved my way through a clutter of progressive hermaphrodites, or whatever they were, and then climbed to the golden sunlight of uptown Manhattan. I had come into a rich district where the shops were vending odd-looking handbags, rare cheeses, and the like. In the window, I saw a dangerous-looking female manikin brandishing a submachine gun. A derelict was vomiting up against the wall. I had to remind myself of the date and city, the century, and that there was definitely something wrong either with me or with 330 million others.

I marched straight ahead to a certain glass and cement building modeled after a sandwich standing on end. I stepped on board a luxurious elevator showing a 3-D movie of a celebrated basketball player doing bumps and grinds. I had forgotten to punch the floor I wanted and had to ride to the top of the building where the door popped open to expose the engines that powered the elevators, as I supposed. A workman, he looked like a workman, was reading a magazine. It was chilly in this part of the building, and a bird, an ordinary wren I believe, was teetering on one of the iron rafters. I was a quarter of a mile up in the sky, one of the last good places in face of rising tides.

"Hello!" said I to the fellow in the split-bottom chair. "Looks like I overshot the mark, ha, ha, ha."

He turned and looked at me. He had a featureless face barely perceptible beneath his MAGA cap.

"Tony send you?" His voice was not antagonistic, and he seemed not at all surprised by my presence in this place. "But you won't be needing those fancy clothes up here."

"I do have some fancy clothes," I told him, "but these are not those. This whole outfit could be had on what you earn in just one day. Tie not included."

He grew suddenly flustered and rose to a standing position. I had been drawing closer to him but now ceased doing so.

"Who told you about that? Hm? You going to answer? Or not?"

"About the tie?"

"About my salary! They're not supposed to talk about stuff like that."

"I'm just trying to get back to the twenty-eighth floor."

"I earn every cent of it."

"No doubt. 'They also serve who sit and wait.'"

"Wordsworth?"

"What the hell, maybe I could just take the staircase."

"Was this Tony's idea? Coming up here dressed like that?"

I now did come nearer, showing him the mediocre quality of my suit. His face was not really without features, though it had been better if it were.

"Coming up here with that piece strapped to your ankle?"

"It's just a Glock."

"Now I get it. You're with the union, right?"

I left him. The area was engorged with machinery and supplies of various kind, and I needed an unbearable time to find the stairs and clamber down the twenty-two floors to the apartment of the anti-Semite said to inhabit the place. I was tired and had to pee, and the prophylactic I wear when traveling was dangerously engorged with the urine already released. The apartment, when I came to it, had a welcoming slogan on the door causing me to jump back an inch or two. Also, there was a tiny frosted window at the top of the door that allowed the tenant(s) to look *out*, provided they be tall enough, but prohibited me looking *in*.

I was admitted into a combination kitchen-bathroom with gingham curtains and a manually-operated can opener, illegal now. My host was a little bit heavier than I like to see in anti-Semites, but his expression was non-committal enough, and the room offered a comfy-looking couch for exhausted visitors to lie upon. But first, I had to rush to the toilet, finding it just in time.

"So. You want to enlist me for an action," he stated factually.

"Are you up for it?"

"Maybe not."

"Alright. Just let me get squared away here and I'll leave you alone." (I made as if I were going to leave him alone.)

"Hold it! Want some coffee? What action are we talking about just exactly?"

"Important action. It's not for everyone. Just some of us."

"It's for you but not necessarily for all of us."

"For me and about thirty others. The best of us."

"When?"

"May 1st."

"This year?"

"Well hell yes this year! Tell me, Paul" (not his real name) "why are you people always trying to delay everything? We'll all be dead eventually."

"The Jews will be dead, too."

"I see. And so, you want them to die *natural* deaths? Did your boy die a natural death defending Israel?"

That did it. He turned and set about pacing the floor. I could hear his footprints entering the back rooms and then coming out again. I flushed the toilet and while waiting for him to resolve himself, prepared a cup of coffee for myself, as I thought it to be.

"Will it be bloody?" he asked innocently.

"Profoundly."

"Oh, Christ. And so, we'll all have to die, too, I suppose."

"Not necessarily. Not necessarily at all. We're in touch with some Black Muslims who will escort us to Fifty-Ninth Street. Provided they get to keep the billfolds and jewelry."

"We don't need the jewelry?"

I had to laugh. He was a good fellow, pretty good, but had always shown himself naïve in these affairs.

"No, we don't need the jewelry. But we'll put a sapphire aside just for you. You know about niggers and how they love sparkly things."

He grinned. I had hooked him by God, and had reeled him in. But did he know how to lock and load and pull a trigger?

In the end, I left him with twenty-five hundred for

weapons and supplies and after complimenting the wife and daughter, Jewish lookalikes both, exited the place at 9:17.

I breakfasted on waffles and sausage and chattered briefly with the waitress, a Hispanic type if ever I had seen one. Her uniform was unclean, but she wore a name tag that told me everything I might need to lodge a complaint later on.

"Gosh," I said, "I don't know how much you're paid, but it can't possibly be enough to compensate for this." (I motioned around at the low-grade clientele.) "However, things are even worse in . . . what? Honduras?"

She smiled. Her hand was as dark as a negro's, and her Aztecan hair was about 95% the color of petroleum. I don't know how long since she had washed it. Her name was easy to remember, but I wrote it down anyway. On the other hand, the coffee was superior, and I sampled two full cups before arising and removing myself. Had she expected a tip? Apparently so, judging from her face seen from the window.

It was a short drive to Queens County, a populous district named after a celebrated ballet dancer. Six weeks before, I had marked my calendar for the criminal trial that ought to be proceeding this day in the Courthouse Adjunct on Eighty-Second Street. I hobbled up the cement stairs of this cement city, detoured around the colored people's water fountain, smiled past the guard, and entered a judicial-looking chamber holding scant people. Nobody cared. The miscreant had murdered his Caucasian cellmate, and only seventeen persons wished to see him hanged and convicted? Hanged indeed, my ole granddaddy would have extracted his spleen with a pair of tweezers.

I managed to seat myself within about twenty to twenty-five feet of the simian, and after verifying that my automatic was in place, semi-automatic, took out a cigarette.

I did not, however, light that cigarette, not at that time. Just a few miles away, my third-favorite opera was performing at the Met. I was aware, too, of the on-going conflict in Kashmir and the mounting death toll over the last days. It is my cross and my splendor that my head never stops spinning.

Himself, the culprit was just about nodding off to sleep. Really, how did it feel to be encased in a bulb-shaped head like his? (Dogs, according to science, don't even know they exist. You can prick an amoeba with a pin and he, [or she] will never know who did it.) The prisoner's cellmate had been good with making peach whiskey, and yet the kaffir had chosen to slay him all the same. Unfortunately for innocent people, his lawyer was Jewish, and the jury was weeping. I wanted to vaporize the lot of them, judge, Jew, jury, and the world along with them.

After this, I left the Annex and ignited that cigarette. Having forgot that I had brought my automobile, I ambulated forward stubbornly against the grain of the onrushing pedestrians. I felt badly for these people, social driftwood hurrying back and forth to create wealth for shareholders. Eaten up with anxiety, allowed to vote, fueled by psychotropic medicines, they saw themselves as the best-situated persons on earth. That was when for one brief moment I thought the rain had come back again.

I detest the city but do love to observe people going about their day in the upper stories of office buildings. I see file clerks earning a living, pretty little creatures saving up for their weddings on the upper stories. I wanted to cry. Life will be good; they are sure of it. Next, returning my attention to ground level, I followed a pair of brood robots holding hands. I noted a heavy woman happily transporting a half-dozen shopping bags. She was a good person, no doubt about it, the best I had seen in weeks, a conscientious wife and mother in a panic to give happiness to whom she loved. At one time—and I know this from personal experience—the country had been full of these. But then, of course, this sight was immediately followed by a divinely-dressed thirty-year-old career girl, ignorant as a cow, in possession of a money-making degree from a snotty school. My ole grandmother could have flayed her alive with two strokes of her bonnet strap.

The weather had turned to snow wherefore I returned to my starting point and got inside my cozy car and locked the doors. Outside, the city was throbbing with business activities of all sorts, but here I could listen to music and smoke in relative safety. It was a pleasant moment which, however, came abruptly to an end when I seemed to have believed that I could view my third wife coming down the street.

In fact, I had been sleeping. Furthermore, I had urinated in my underwear, and it was only with difficulty that I was able to get into my reserve trousers without presenting a scene to the passersby. I got into clean socks, fastened my ankle holster, and then carefully relinquished my parking space to a militant-looking jigaboo with dreads and a golden necklace. But where now, if I may ask again, was my dear dead grandfather who had disposed of a fair number of such elements during his all-too-brief tenure on earth?

Fifteen

The traffic was hideous, of course, but eventually I came into a flat region where I could begin to move out ahead of the women driving at their usual speed. One of these was crying, one was drunk, and one appeared normal. I accelerated to about fifty knots and passed them by. It was 1:02 in the early afternoon and a great sadness enveloped just about everything. The office workers were scurrying to return to work before too late. They had come to town to contribute to the economy, squandering four times as many work-hours as needed for a cultured life. Here in this envied city, the people spent more time at traffic lights than with their spouses. I've seen some of those spouses.

Such sadness and such a long time before history will expunge this age and splice the West back together again. So much sadness and such a density of sulfate fumes. To-day, the clouds looked like Confederate generals. I came up even with a roadside dog, a tattered creature able to find neither food nor water in the world's richest city. To bark would incur the death penalty.

My destination, of course, was Vermont, a district psy-chologically nearer to me at that time than Alabama itself. Rumors had arrived of a Montpelier man recently let out of prison on DNA evidence proving that he could not pos-sibly have murdered seven Jews all at one time. Contacted by Reece, the man allowed coyly that perhaps it was more possible than widely believed. Received he then, the killer, a spate of electronic mail that authorized him to com-municate with our group from long distance. Recruitment had fallen off lately, and we needed another four-hundred to five-hundred members to bring us back to "critical mass," as Taw called it.

My exhilaration increased as my car and I plowed ea-gerly through the outlying slops of the city. I had put Mussorgsky's *Death Songs* on the machine, portentous music that sorted well with the coming of spring. An hour and a half later, we broke free of the chemical odors that sheltered New York City on all sides. A long time had gone past since last I had smelt the smell of grass and trees and, it even seemed to me, flowers and magnolia trees. No, but I really could pick up a hint of things not emanating from cities.

Moving quickly, I ran through the tiny city of Gelt-bridge, famous for a historical reason not familiar to me. Would Vermont be different, and would the men stroll as slowly and proudly as God intended? Would I find boys in straw hats carrying fishing poles over their shoulders? Stop it. That was when I belatedly recognized that I had but very little fuel still remaining to me; even so, I continued on for a few more miles before verging off into a digitized service station offering various grades of solar fuels.

It wasn't so long ago that my Saxon Touring Car would have created a sensation among gasoline service station attendants, another old-time occupation voided by automation. Hesitantly, I punched the buttons, spoke, and right away the hose emerged from above and came to hand. But first, I had to watch a brief, fairly brief film promoting a chain of clothing stores. Came then a voice telling me to protect my eyes from the sun and to report people using tobacco products. I had selected a medium-grade fuel mixed with extract. The stuff did do what was wanted, however, and proved able to propel me forward at slightly above the legal speed.

We came into a town, the car and I, of perhaps fifteen to twenty-thousand souls, a place too small for opera houses and too large for a cultivated person. I did *not* stop for coffee, not after I caught sight of the customers sitting hip-to-hip behind a plate-glass window. There might be a good person in that lot, there might be two, but I didn't wish to chance my life on a bet like that. I was listening to Ravel's *Daphnis and Chloe* when I was forced to stop for a yellow school bus unloading all sorts of underage Daphnises and Chloes to go scurrying homeward with their school equipment. There was nothing wrong with these children; it might almost have been 1950 all over again. But I knew, even if their lackadaisical parents did not, what lay ahead for them. I wanted to stop them in mid-stride as they dashed forward to be embraced by their dogs and mothers.

The next town had an appealing aspect at first, which is to say until my eye beams collided into a 300 to 325-pound white (!) lady skiing down the pavement on splayed feet. I could have deflated her with a pointed toothpick but didn't actually have one. I did see, and I admit this, a few people seemingly worthy of the beauty of this state. But hardly had I said those words (for the benefit of my future biographers) when I caught sight of a deranged man of some description companioning a bright yellow Chinese in tattoos and a baseball cap. Leaving the place behind, I broke into a twenty-mile stretch of shopping centers. I slowed and stopped and tried to analyze the faces of those coming in and out. Some say floods, some asteroid strike, but I believe the world ends with merchandizing.

To make a short report shorter, I did arrive in northwest Vermont just before dark. It's the contrast between this lovely place and its property owners that sends me to despair. A meet place for philosophers and Right-wing authors, the place had been preempted by consumers, college professors, hockey fans, government agents, and the like. Here, I loitered a few moments to watch a saffron sun, ten times larger than it ought to be, threatening the world's finest horizon. Just imagine, said I, *she* were with me now!

I peed, emptied the jar, and turned my nose toward the walled city of Montpelier. I halted for the toll taker (who examined my face with undisguised dislike) and then handed him the entry fee together with a fairly appreciable gratuity. For those of you still following this account, I would, in fact I do, describe him as an atrabilious personality who had been stationed in one place for much too long. The town itself seemed reasonable enough as I probed the circumferential streets before then plunging into the heart of this northeastern setup. They jeered at my car, of course, the sidewalk youth. But negroes were few and far between, a state of affairs beneficial for the cityscape. Hiding my cigarette, I drove slowly past a succession of boutiques, flea markets, puppet shows, and other

businesses dear to the hearts of the bohemian rich. Somewhere inside this maze my destination lay. I dislike relying
on geodetic gizmos, but with night drawing on, I relented
one more time. Lights were coming on all over Vermont.

I turned into Jeb Stuart Street, went to the next intersection, and stopped. Before actually knocking at the
door, I needed to surveil the house and contents of this
self-identified Aryan who might in fact have been a provo-
cateur salaried to unmask those of us. Taking my MPQ
Resonator from its place, I was given a bird's eye view of
the place via an invisible roof. He was an exceptionally fat
individual, somewhat fat, half-asleep in a red-leather sofa
with a paisley cushion beneath his tetrahedral but astute-
looking head. I homed in upon the book that had fallen to
the floor and was able, barely, to read the title of that dis-
reputable treatise. No one else was within the house, not
at that moment at any rate. A structure of five rooms only,
I estimated its market value as of just six or maybe six and
a half million Euro. Nor were the contents of his refrigerator especially encouraging. But instead of finetuning my
device to identify its contents, I secreted my weapon under my belt and proceeded to the home itself.

It needed an ungodly time for the rectum to come to
the door. His own weapon was a revolver of some kind.
Appareled in a fringed robe, he bowed in my direction,
squinting painfully into the night. Followed then about
five seconds followed by others. His slippers were in woe-
ful condition.

"G'morning!" I called out cheerfully, my left hand quite
prepared to draw and shoot. "But is it good for the Jews?"

I was escorted into a largish well-arranged room that
was notably in need of furniture. In the age-long competition between thrift and comfort, he had chosen the first-
mentioned. Excellent; I liked him already. Better, he had a
terrarium of unusual size, inside it some demonic-looking
specimens with snagged teeth. I had about as soon dip my

hand into that milieu as be sued by a Jewish lawyer.

But before engaging in actual conversation with this person, I asked permission to inspect his floor-to-ceiling bookcase that continued over into the next room. He loved the Greeks—good. He knew something about the Medieval Age, too, and possessed a fine collection by and about the Desert Fathers, Saint Anthony particularly. He had a treatise in manuscript form concerning garden-grown poisons as also a sales catalog of the Sig Sauer company. He had a complete set of Kratverskaya in Russian, and, in short, I admired the man without further hesitation.

"*Everything*," he said, "is for the Jews. Or till we can straighten things out."

"And when will that be?"

"You tell me. That's why I invited you here."

I smiled, unusual for me, and ignited a cigarette. "Well, sir," I said, inhaling deeply and blowing it out again, "we can *begin* to do something on May 1st."

"May 1st?"

"Yes. That's the day we send out the first issue of our new journal."

"Do I get one?"

"Not 'less you join us."

"Join?"

"Precisely. We don't ask much—just that you help us slaughter about twenty or possibly thirty small dark Yids leaving their temple, they call it."

"Thirty?"

"If God be with us. Are you up for that?"

"*Thirty*, you said?"

"Could be a thousand if the wind is just right."

"Thirty. And I've only ever done six."

We supped on groceries and a few other things washed down with maple syrup. I asked for more of that famous Vermont product, and he obliged by providing me a bib and tucker and then spooning perhaps a dozen ounces of the matter into my waiting maw. It had a mischievous quality, and the flux was better than wine. I detected a copy of the celebrated 1940 photograph of Houston Chamberlain on the facing wall. He had been married at one time, my host, as I judged from the stand-up portrait on the mantelpiece.

"My second wife," he described.

"And best one, too, I'll warrant."

"We used to . . ."

"I know, I know."

This good man had a pool table in the adjoining room with a mouse residing in the corner pocket. Apparently, he had not played in a long time, and I was easily able to defeat him in the only two games we played. He took it well, laughed easily, paid promptly, and came back with the spoon and syrup.

"Alright. How?" he asked finally.

I told him about that synagogue up on Ninety-Ninth Street. "Two billionaires in that crowd. A State Senator, pawnbroker, two jewelers and the preeminent pornographer in the Northeast."

"Okay. I'm in."

I slept acceptably well that night and then woke at just after nine. We had waffles and syrup and together went over his weaponry and ammunition. He owned two long guns, one of them much the better, and almost a pound of 5.56 ammunition. I would have preferred, did prefer, and still do prefer heavier equipment. I acknowledge what ordnance of that kind can accomplish in able hands, namely turn to absolute goo what a moment earlier had been human glands.

"Tell me," I demanded, "how you learned about the Jews."

"I was young."

"Go on."

"And I was working at this advertising place where everybody was a Jew."

"But not you. You weren't a Jew, were you?"

"Not at that time."

"And now?"

"No."

"Go on. You don't have to stop speaking after each sentence for Christ's sakes."

"Well, we used to close up for lunch and then go into that room back there, the one on the left where they had these folders and file cabinets and so forth."

"I'm waiting."

"Well, we used to have lunch back there and I guess they forgot I weren't a Jew, too. The food was pretty good. They used to get stains on those great big glasses they wear. That's why they have those noses I guess, to hold those glasses up."

He laughed at the joke.

"Well, they used to talk about people like us" he continued. "All the time."

"Let me guess: they want us dead."

"No. No, I don't think so. No, they want us to stay alive so's we can work for 'em. Because they're smarter than us."

I grabbed for my semi-automatic, capsizing my coffee as I did so. He went on:

"But then one day, I fell off that ladder . . ."

"Ladder?"

"Yeah. It was broken, and I fell down. Fifteen feet near about. That's why I have to wear these braces."

"You didn't receive any compensation for that fall, I presume."

"Naw. They got me to sign these papers. But they gave me a glass of water."

"Could you recognize these people?"

"Well, one of 'em was short and had a scrunched-up face."

"To be sure. Others?"

"Well, there was this one person. But I found out where he lived and killed him dead already."

I swooned.

Readers should, too.

Sixteen

Time was wasting and meantime spring was coming in. On April 3rd, I detected an inch-tall sprig of what might have been a dandelion emerging from the third crack in the sidewalk that led to my apartment house door. Skirts were getting shorter. The girls were in season, and the nights were shorter, too.

I darkened my windows in aluminum foil and did a fair amount of reading during that time to honor forgotten authors. Did I really expect to die on May 1st? Not really. All my life I've been a slippery sort of individual, and I was confident, somewhat confident that I'd be able to pass myself off as one of the ambulance drivers when the time came around. I composed one, two, three letters to my favorite ex-wife and left them in my safe-deposit box. I organized my pharmaceuticals, arranging them by increasing strength up until the day. One sole anti-Semite was still lingering in my basement, but I was able to send him to France on a not-very-difficult mission. He was far too timorous in spirit to share in our approaching task.

April 18th, I rented a twenty-foot storage shelter just outside Jamaica City and had it fitted with throw-away bookcases bought cheaply from run-down antique outlets. And then over the next few days, I paid a negro dummkopf to relocate to that place nearly all my books, music recordings, microscope, family albums, pills, cuff links, and Tamayo's *Three Musicians*, the only original oil in my possession. Let this show how willing was I to die on behalf of a supernal cause. Let it be said, too, that on the twentieth I received a highly unexpected visit from my *first* wife, a very different sort of individual as compared and contrasted to my second spouse.

"Regina!" I called out. "How did you get my address? Come on in, come on in. If you want to, I mean."

She had not aged especially well. Good with make-up, she might still have passed for sixty, however. She opted to come inside. She had been a shapely creature at one time, very much less so now.

"It happens to us all," I said. "Need a drink?"

"No, no, I just wanted to touch base."

(And will she wish to touch base again after another twenty-five years have gone by?)

"Excellent. How's the boy?" (That's right people, I had had a boy in the old days, a jewel in the crown of mediocrity.) "Still in business, is he?"

"Oh, I suppose. He was in Philadelphia for a while."

"Married?"

"Me? No, Teddy and I separated long ago. I still see David from time to time."

"Jew?"

She laughed. "Well, I can see you haven't changed! No, I think he's a . . . Oh, I don't know. He's involved in lots of things"

"A Jew. Ready for that drink now?"

The rum was gone wherefore I served her with an absinth chilled with frozen cubes composed also of absinth. A stalwart drink, she had no hesitation in decanting a third of it with the first draught. Owing to varicose veins, her hosiery was dark. She had been a desirable female at one period but now was as obsolete as your reporter. Nor was her dentition a cause for celebration, not when a ray of sunlight broke through that gap between the curtains and illuminated for a moment the interior of her mouth. Should have been euthanized ten years ago, this woman.

"How are your finances holding up these days?" I asked, wanting to preempt the issue. "Hard times, these!

Never thought I'd actually have to borrow money to pay my mortgage."

"You paid cash! Everybody knows that."

"Another drink?"

We chatted for an hour, but she didn't get a dime. What, I'm supposed to assist those two former wives of mine who never filled even the most elementary of my requirements? While ignoring the one whose simplest and most justifiable requests I never granted? I'm supposed to keep myself apprised of the economic activities of my purported son? Supposed to remember the district court judgement against me?

She left me at just after three whereupon I prepared a largish Tom Collins and over the course of about half an hour drank it down to the grinds. By the time I had finished and had enjoyed a good sleep, it was two days later and my chameleons were furious. I could tell from the noise that a new guest had taken up in the East Room though I opted not to interview him at this time.

Night came and none too soon. I paid my overdue bills, thirty-two of them, and had a drink. No significant rain in a week or more. Instead of rising, the ocean would soon be so low I'd be able to pilfer shipwrecks wearing galoshes only. I tuned in to "The Market," America's spiritual center, to find that I had lost twenty-one thousand dollars. Molybdenum futures were doing fine, however. Today, the news was being presented by a blond woman of perhaps thirty-five years, the clone of half a dozen other blue-chip presenters in good clothes. And now, I must venture into Manhattan once again.

Because a new production of *Parsifal* was premiering. The singers were good, pretty good, excellent actually and included a soprano of elephantine stature. Suffering from a Jewish boycott, the event needed my adherence. Gretel declined to accompany me, however.

I was to walk a mile, approximately (I needed the exercise) and then flag down a ride on the Long Island Railroad. Next, I was to transfer to the befitting subway station and ride a little distance further. I would then stroll about three hundred yards and arrive, hopefully, in time to have a sloe gin fizz prior to curtain time. I was excited.

And in truth, I did all these things. I walked my mile, ordered my sloe, and caught up at the last moment with the next following subway car. I had learned earlier in my New York career that one need not pay for a ticket if that person continues to stroll from one car to the next and then back again. (One does not necessarily want a seat in any case for fear of the person he might be sitting with. This was the present situation.) I stood therefore, pretending to be thinking. It appalled me that even here one of the new iterations of "Green Hornet" drones was chasing alongside the train at eye level. A black man came on board at the next stop, but I was able to shift my wallet quickly to my vest. We looked at each other. They know, these people, when a person wears an ankle holster.

Two stops further, a frightened-looking woman and her children tried to get on board. The children succeeded. Ahead, the grey city loomed like a tsunami poised to wash Long Island out to sea. Plunging forward into that quark-gluon plasma, we call it, an intense headache was gathering force down deep in my sub-cortex. The richest city in the world, soon to be a neglected archeological site. I discerned aggressive lichens advancing up the apartment buildings, a man in an athletic supporter sitting on a window sill, and a good deal else. This be my interpretation of New York City.

In accord with my itinerary, I went from train to subway at the corner of Nathan Forrest and MLK. I'll admit there were some worrisome figures waiting at the platform, but I was able to throw myself without incident into the first available car. I took a seat next to an elderly white man pretending to be sleeping. He seemed glad to see me.

Together, we had some chance at least to hold off any ordinary negro. As mentioned, I had my Glock, and my friend carried a stick.

We pushed forward at high speed through a blinking neon tunnel with startling invitations inscribed on the walls. I caught a fleeting glimpse of a dignified-looking man in a suit emerge stealthily from one of the tunnels. Just then, we ran over an obstacle of about the size of a man or dog. The passengers hardly noticed. I examined the faces of my fellow travelers, finding just two who passed my personal muster. And how were things down south, and the girls, were they just as demur? I daren't go and look.

I abandoned the subway at 6:32, climbed to street level, hurried to the nearest department store, and pushed my way to the men's facility. Unwilling to accompany me so far, my friend from the subway had turned and gone back. It was not a pleasant place, the facility, but did give me a chance to urinate in peace and replace the prophylactic that was near to bursting. Someone in one of the stalls was yelping in pain. City dwellers are a Jewish people, and the water in my urinal was tinctured with a fluid of some nature. Acting quickly, I flushed it out of sight and out of mind.

My next job was to find a drinking place and get me a high-octane drink of some sort. But the place, when I found it, was invested with smiling girls deliriously happy to be out and about and enjoined in conversations with others of the same kind. Human celery, bland as water thrice distilled. Surely, surely one of these persons had experienced a thought at one time, or had yearned, or had looked life straight in the face. I preferred the bartender, a brutal-looking manifestation who might actually know a thing or two.

I wedged up to the bar, forcing two college girls to make space for me. But my drink was slow to arrive, and when it did the stuff had already separated. Absinth una-vailable, I accepted what was given. The girl on my right was gaily bedight in a pale blue sweater holding twin bos-oms of real capacity. Somewhere, one of tomorrow's un-married doctors or lawyers was thinking of her just now. Turning toward her courteously, I said:

"Hello."

"Hi."

"Say something intelligent, Okay?"

She collected her purse and drink and abandoned her stool to me, which I accepted. For those of us about to die, no rules apply.

Seventeen

Tuesday the 25th, I bathed and shaved, put on my fa-vorite tie and after reading briefly in our new journal, fell asleep on the toilet. But mostly, my time was for preparing our "last supper," we called it, and setting up reservations in the back room of The Pied Cow, our dedicated meeting place these days. The proprietor, a mid-level anti-Semite, is a dear friend of ours, but even so we had to put down a considerable deposit against the chance of interference by the police, Jews, journalists, and anti-white cadres gener-ally. For our defense, the Finn and I had secreted five semi-automatics among the tables and chairs. Gretel would be there, and I was not so certain that my first wife mightn't also appear. I had organized a showing of *Der Ewige Jude,* a resonating movie seldom viewed in New York City.

With all things made right, I devoted Wednesday to music and revisiting the first four chapters of Victor Glab's brilliant anti-Semitic *The Vile People* in which the Ashke-nazi genome is diagrammed in full detail. Brave though I am, I slept poorly that night, overly excited by the imag-ined sound of Confederate artillery moving near. Should I be killed on the following day, where would they invest my remains? That was when I leapt up suddenly, went to my pen and paper and described the Alabama cemetery in which I wished to be laid. I mentioned the books to be added to the coffin, the painting of my second wife, her letters, and the recording (locked away in an ant-free time-capsule) of a talk given by me at a recent riot attended by reporters from *The New York Skeptic*. I shall describe these requirements to my Fifth Avenue lawyer who has so often shown that he knows how to accomplish what is asked.

The dawn was unpromising, the sun no brighter than a leaden penny bearing an eroded text. I was nervous. With no rain portending, I opted to go out into the street and look at people. I took the risk of igniting a cigarette, hardly bothering to hide the thing. A hundred yards from home, I espied a normal-looking woman whom I followed for a short distance before then turning back to feed my livestock. The smallest of the chameleons had turned green with annoyance, and his tail appeared to be peeling. We looked at each other.

To those who have followed this account up until this time, I express my amazement and delight. No, I do not ask and do not expect to see these hastily-written but luminescent paragraphs put into book form and sold for actual money. Unless you want to. Among my papers you will find a list of those who should inherit my books, cuff links, my Byzantine coin, and other money. My lizards cannot, of course, subsist in New York's outdoor weather for which reason I have instructed that they be forwarded to my second wife, packaging instructions to follow.

I fuddled away the hours between ten and five, listened to Abravenal's rendition of Mahler's Eighth while taking care to skip over the appalling first movement, an excrementitious exercise not worth hearing. I had prepared a covered dish of sweet potatoes and marshmallows for our banquet, having determined in advance that our anti-Semitic host would keep it warm. I then called Gretel to be certain she'd be there, reminding her to bring the fudge. My second wife wasn't able to answer her telephone.

The restaurant was not so far away, and I chose to walk the distance, holding my sweet potatoes level in the dish. How ironic if the rain should select *this* time to make up for the past two weeks of dearth. But no, it remained dry, mostly dry, throughout the twenty-minute stroll. The sun meantime had turned edgewise, as it almost seemed, offering scant warmth to the huddled masses down below. Leaving a discontinuous trail of blood on the pavement, an ambulance ran past followed by a score of lawyers in long black cars. The stock market had been down all day long, and that, together with the sun, had done nothing to enliven the world's most seminal city. My prophylactic was half-full by now, and with the clock approaching five o'clock, the office workers were abandoning their work stations in hundreds and more. Let just one of those well-dressed businesspersons collide into my potatoes and I'll draw my gun.

It pleased me to find that Taw had arrived already. Having visited the latrine, I deposited my sweet potatoes on the table alongside his chicken wings and went to shake with him. In his sloppy penmanship, he had been drafting the remarks he proposed to offer once the group had come together. He had never wanted to be the leader of our organization, the chief reason we would accept no other.

"Hey!" said I. "It's been a while."

"Since we last talked?"

"Yes. And had a drink together."

"Ah, Lord. Truth is, I don't drink anymore."

"Sorry to hear it. Why?"

"It was making me older."

He did not look much older, not as old as me. And in fact, he wasn't as old as me.

"You don't look so old. Are you still doing pushups?"

"Ah, Christ. I used to do fifteen. Now I can scarce do half that many."

"Want to hear how many *I* can do?"

"Just so long as you can still pull the trigger on that Glock of yours."

God, I liked that man. And if he and I are still living when you see this, I like him still. He has silver hair and a noble profile, and I dread to think what a policeman's bullet might do to him on tomorrow day.

"I wonder if it might not have been just as well to use explosives," I mooted.

"No. No, I don't think so. Explosives lack that personal touch. You want to *see* the Jews you're killing."

"The expression on their faces?"

"Yes. That's why I'm going to ask the fellows to aim for the belly instead of the head. That's where the pain is."

He had little wrinkles about the eyes that reflected delight when he pronounced the pain word. Fred had meantime arrived bringing a blonde item of perhaps one-third his age and size. We had spoken to him about this but apparently, he hadn't been able to contain his motives regarding that gender. Taw offered him a chicken wing which he accepted and washed down with two intakes of the brown ale the proprietor had contributed.

"Well," he said—(we're talking about Fred now)—"I reckon tomorrow's the day we die."

"No!" his girlfriend supplied.

We feasted on several kinds of beans while Alois, having dined already, entertained us with his baritone clarinet. He was a good instrumentalist, pretty good, and the tunes were from the superannuated repertoire most familiar to us. I do not hold with the popular music produced after the 1950s, nor should you. I begged Gretel to sing (though I knew she wouldn't) but did finally manage to cajole Fred's woman to do the job instead. Her voice was what it was, and she used it unembarrassedly.

I haven't even begun to described the food. Having finished with it, we helped the women gather up the dishes and then stood by as they brought out the coffee and tarts with cherries on them. I was weary of being served by salaried waitresses; by comparison, these anti-Semitic girls seemed to add flavor to everything they fetched. It would have been useless to try and pinch Gretel's rear end, and in any case, I grabbed for it much too late. Finally, we all lit up cigars or cigarettes and pushed back to listen to Taw. He stood, brushed the crumbs from his lap, and began to talk. He didn't want to be there.

"I would have wanted someone else to do this . . ." he started out.

"*Would have wanted*? Or do want?"

It was Frank, or Rank Frank as we called him, far the most persnickety man among us on matters grammatical. We hooted him down but not before he had flustered Taw, a man far greater than Frank himself. We waited for our selected leader to regain himself.

"But no one else wanted to do it."

"Hear, hear!" we cried. "Keep talking."

"Well," he said, "the Jews won't leave the synagogue till twelve or thereabouts but we need to . . ."

"A.m.? Or p.m.?"

We hooted him down. We might actually have ejected the hound, had he not brought 500 rounds of 5.56 ammo. He was (is) a good marksman, too, as well we knew. If he is still breathing as you read this, I emphatically recommend him for future actions, all else notwithstanding. Taw went on:

". . . need to be there at about 11:30. Larry," (not his real name) "and his sons will be on the roof of that hardware across the street. That will give them a perfect line of sight into the crowd. Meanwhile, Jimmy will use his night-vision goggles to aim into the vestibule that's likely to be dark. We realize that many of these elements will try to escape out the side door, but we'll block that with Toby's pick-up. And if any of them do manage to squeeze out of the cracks, we have people ready to blow them apart. Not one single kike will get away, I promise you."

Applause. He went on speaking:

"I believe we can kill at least twenty of these people before the police know about it. Maybe thirty. And if we can get *inside* the place, we can finish them off without trouble. All our weapons have silencers, even the shotguns. But if the police *do* learn about it? I knew someone would ask that question. Remember, we don't want to kill any more policemen than absolutely necessary. They don't like stuff like that."

"And after? What about after?"

"Well, as if I haven't already made it clear, and I think I have, our Black Muslim friends are going to be waiting in eleven Lincoln Town Cars parked both on this side of the street and on the other. Get into the nearest car and fasten your seat belt."

"Where are they taking us?"

"Bring a damp towel so you can wash the gun powder off your face. And *do not* take off your gloves, not till we get to where we're going."

"Where?"

We gave our leader a standing ovation. The women released large tears that ended up either on the floor or in their deserts. Someone opened champagne, and I was the first person not to refuse any. Taw continued:

"And now the time has come to introduce my dear friend Mikey Blissit."

It was the man's real name as we learned later. We also learned later, or soon thereafter, why he had no fear of revealing it. He was indeed an elderly sort of hominid with very long grey hair that gave him the transgressive look of a nonagenarian motorcycle rider. He came forward and waved at us while Taw provided his biography. A motorcycle rider in truth, this maladjusted individual had studied at Heidelberg, had produced with the aid of a test-tube a son with a big I.Q. But just a year and a half prior to this time, he had contracted a liver cancer that proposed to kill him before next summertime. He grinned. His teeth were in awful condition, but it was far too late to worry about that. Taw held his hand, Mikey's, up in the air and went on talking:

"Don't worry about those teeth; he's going to die anyway. But more importantly, he's going to be wearing a vest full of GPT explosives strong enough to *bring that whole fucking building down!*"

You can probably imagine the delirium that followed. The cheers must have gone on for a full seven or eight minutes, becoming louder as time went past. Gretel rushed to him, leaving lipstick on his purplish mouth. One of the young ones actually pulled the man's gun and shot into the air. And so, it had come to this, that we and a few others like us stood as both the last and the best hindrance to the collapse of the West.

I strolled homeward, accompanying Rodney as far as Seventy-Second Street. Here we parted, he to continue to his hovel in the Portuguese district and I to my excessively well-appointed headquarters further east. Referencing the parting words of Brutus in Shakespeare's *Julius Caesar*, he embraced me warmly and then turned and went his way. Either we would never meet again, or else we would. In the former case, we would have nothing more to say to each other while in the other case we might very well see each other again in the place to which the Mohammedans would take us. Feeling as I do about Rodney, I would be just as happy not to meet him evermore again.

It was a long, dark, very dark and lonely walk I undertook that night. Down below, I could pick up the noise of subway trains running back and forth with their odious cargoes. A far-eastern Gook of some nationality was lingering in the mouth of the alley but I warded him off quite easily with my Glock. Not far away, the Soccer Stadium was all aglow, this new spate of public executions redounding importantly to the fiscal welfare of the ticket sellers. Uniquely for New York City, I could see perhaps half a dozen stars blinking in the assumed sky.

I dared to step into a coffee bar but then quickly stepped out again. Instead of negroes, I had intruded into a gathering of exceptionally well-dressed New York career women laughing into one another's faces. Eroticized by the sight of each other, they wished to delay as long as possible returning to their spouses. First, we do the Jews, and these later.

Final

I arrived home just in time to go to sleep. The contents of my aquarium had been given away, but I could still hear the last of the anti-Semites arguing in the basement. There was, of course, no chance of sleep this night, very likely the last such night of my current impersonation. I called my second wife, let it ring for four seconds, and then decided not to bother her at this time. I covered the remains of the sweet potatoes in wax paper and nudged them to the back of the bottom shelf of my Japanese-made refrigerator. I drank. Perhaps too much, and then put on the MacIntosh interpretation of Mahler's *Abschied*.

Very many times in the past, I've been able to access mentally my remembered list of early dreams and replay them even when half-asleep. But not tonight. My friends, too, I had to suppose, were turning in their beds. To find surcease, I switched on the television to six commercials starring respectively an immense black bear striving to steal honey, a lovely girl in a bathtub, an elfin sort of individual conjuring a certain brand of hair oil, and three other productions of like significance. I do wish Socrates might have seen this before he died. Apparently, I did sleep briefly, dreaming that just outside my window I saw a small green toad riding athwart a bat.

Ah, well. Slowly and begrudgingly, I packed my bags—my disassembled 30-06 deer rifle, my Smith & Wesson with laser lights, my bulletproof vest (of small value against big ammunition), my suicide tablets, morphine and bandages, all of it. The entire mess weighs above thirty-two pounds, but I'm not yet so old that I can't manage it. That was when Taw called. He couldn't sleep, of course, but nevertheless considered himself qualified to bolster *my* waning courage.

"Someday," I said, "you might be in charge of this whole country."

"Rather be dead."

"So, who will lead us then?"

"Hasn't been born yet. Now you try and get some sleep, you hear?"

"How about Fred Reeves?"

"Don't think so. But if *you* want him . . ."

"Lord, no. How about the new fellow?"

"We can discuss this at a later time, don't you think?"

"If we survive, you mean."

"Right. Okay, I'll see you at about 11:30, okay?"

"Absolutely. Taw?"

"Yes?"

"What's it going to be like?"

"Don't forget the pills."

I peed five times that night, and then at 4:00 placed my three best chameleons in separate jars, watered them, and carried them down to the park. No chance they'd survive a New York winter, of course, but in the nonce they might at least get their meed of sun.

ABOUT THE AUTHOR

Tito Perdue was born in 1938 in Chile, the son of an electrical engineer from Alabama. The family returned to Alabama in 1941, where Tito graduated from the Indian Springs School, a private academy near Birmingham, in 1956. He then attended Antioch College in Ohio for a year, before being expelled for cohabitating with a female student, Judy Clark. In 1957, they were married, and remain so today. He graduated from the University of Texas in 1961, and spent some time working in New York City, an experience which garnered him his life-long hatred of urban life. After holding positions at various university libraries, Tito has devoted himself full-time to writing since 1983.

His first novel, 1991's *Lee,* received favorable reviews in *The New York Times, The Los Angeles Reader*, and *The New England Review of Books*. In addition to the present volume, his novels include *The New Austerities* (1994), *Opportunities in Alabama Agriculture* (1994), *The Sweet-Scented Manuscript* (2004), *Fields of Asphodel* (2007), *The Node* (2011), *Morning Crafts* (2013), *Reuben* (2014), the *William's House* quartet (2016), *Cynosura* (2017), *Philip* (2017), *Though We Be Dead, Yet Our Day Will Come* (2018), *The Bent Pyramid* (2018), *The Philatelist* (2018), *The Smut Book* (2018), *The Gizmo* (2019), and *Material for All Future Historians* (2019)—which have been praised in *Chronicles: A Magazine of American Culture, The Quarterly Review, The Occidental Observer*, and at *Counter-Currents*.

In 2015, he received the H. P. Lovecraft Prize for Literature.